HUNG

ANNE MARSH

Copyright © 2017 Anne Marsh
All rights reserved.

1

PICK

Y OU know those *how I met your mother* stories? Where he looks at her and she looks at him, the birds start warbling *Ode to Joy*, and Mother Nature lights the whole scene up with a gorgeous fucking sunset?

Ask me how I met Sarah Jo.

Go on. You know you want to.

I'll give you three guesses.

She was the porn star fielding my 1-900 call, you suggest? Not a chance. I don't have to pay for sex.

Not gonna lie—it's tempting because then there are no misunderstandings or hurt feelings. I'm just renting hot, wet space and treating my dick to the manly version of a spa day.

Don't be offended. I've never pretended to be a gentleman—or to have a filter. If the thought enters my head, it comes out my mouth. You take the good with the bad, and my super-sized, XXXL dick package and my filter-less mouth have an until-death-do-us-part relationship.

So take your second guess and cut me some slack. Blind date? *Please.* I'm too busy fighting fires to have time to date, plus there's a singular lack of attractive, unattached women in Big Bear Lake. In fact, we're dick central and we could use way more women in this particular part of Northern California. Some enterprising soul could make a fortune delivering mail-order girlfriends to my very horny teammates. Single women get plenty of dating action here. It's a small town, not a wide selection. No one fixed me up with Sarah Jo. I didn't take her out for a steak the size of her head or a bottle of not-inexpensive red wine. We didn't dance, didn't dine, didn't exchange an awkward first kiss outside her door when I brought her home.

She tried to bash my head in with a baseball bat.

I'll let you think about that for a minute.

I meet the girl of my dreams and she takes her best shot at killing me.

Buckle up, sit tight, and hang on for the ride because Sarah Jo and I are about to go lights and sirens. I'm on my way to Baby Bear Lodge to rescue one of my hotshot team members. He's been sucked into the orbit of this crazy group of chicks who run something called the Break Up Club. For all you guys out there, that means they get together and roast us. Talk over all our shortcomings, compare dick stories, and set shit on fire. Being wiser (if not older) than Hunter, I've opted for the local titty bar over the local cabal, but I need another wingman and I've nominated Hunter in absentia. He's relatively new both to town and to the hotshot team, so he may have overlooked the merits of taking the look-but-don't-touch approach to life. Dragging him with me to watch half-naked girls gyrating on a stage is a kindness.

Not that the bar looks all that exciting from the outside. It's one more dumpy, run-down building by the highway. The road slows to a meander where it passes through Big Bear Lake, with speeds dropping to a miserly thirty miles per hour. Still, if you blink, you'll miss *Tits Up*. Some decorating genius painted it the perfect shade of brown to blend into the landscape, and nothing announces that you've just found a man haven. In fact, the only thing *Tits Up* had going for it is the obvious pair (or pairs) of things. Lots of boobs, lots of shaking and shimmying, and no need to talk.

My team singlehandedly keeps the place in business, officially because it's the only bar with a full liquor license. The alternative is *Drink Up* (Big Bear Lake's founding fathers showed a lamentable lack of creativity in their naming). The bar is only allowed to serve beer, although they bend the rules for those weird beer-margarita hybrids that come in a can. Let's just say that a pop-top cannot replace the salty goodness of icy cold tequila and leave it at that.

By the time Colt pulls into the driveway at Baby Bear Lodge, however, I'm rethinking my plans for the evening. This is because the man was doing a hundred and twenty not thirty seconds ago. I've got whiplash from the slow-down. No ride to the bar is worth this kind of trauma. Colt shoves his cowboy hat back and folds his arms on the steering wheel, laughing like a hyena.

"I coulda gone faster," he points out. "You need

a barf bag?"

Har-de-har-har. Serve him right if I puke into that stupid hat he's so attached to.

"Fuck you," I grunt, fumbling for the door handle. I'm sure the ladies love his dimples but right now I just want to punch the shit out of him. If he went any faster, we'd be in fucking orbit right now. I have no idea how Adrian can still be asleep on the backseat.

"Seriously?" The stupid dimples in Colt's face get deeper. "You ready to take our relationship to the next level?"

I concentrate on sucking in some air. It's way easier to breathe now I'm not watching the hairpin turns in the mountain highway leap out of the dark at me.

You need someone to jump out of a plane into a fire? I'm your guy. Hike twenty miles into a wildfire and then play hide-and-seek with the flames? Again, I'm totally onboard. I've been singed with the best of them, have pushed my luck time and time again. Doing a hundred and twenty down the highway, however, isn't my idea of a good time. Letting Colt volunteer to drive was a rookie mistake. The man's a former racecar driver and he thinks doing sixty is like sitting in the slow lane with your thumb up your ass. Some people enjoy the backdoor action but it's not his thing.

On the other hand, we did get here in record time.

So I settle for flipping him the bird and muttering an amiable *fuck off* as I swing down from his truck. He can't even drive a normal truck—his is jacked about a million feet into the air on oversized tires that could crush the contents of your average Walmart parking lot and keep right on driving.

"You need a hand extricating our boy?"

I wave a hand and trudge up the drive. In a moment of genius, we decided that Colt would park at the bottom of the driveway so as not to alert Hunter to our presence. Not that the guy has anywhere to run to— the whole driveway's blocked thanks to Colt's monster truck. And just in case I really thought the stealth approach was the way to go, Colt gets busy changing the tunes. I wasn't the only one miserable on the drive over since I made him listen to what he calls my "classical shit." Colt claims that's why he had to drive so fast. I claim he has no taste. Now country music blasts from the speakers, some dude whining about how he can't live without this girl he just spotted in a bar, his bed, his best friend's bed—I can't keep track of that shit.

I hoof it to the top of the driveway double-time. The closer I get, the clearer it becomes that keeping my own noise down isn't necessary. The Break Up Club girls are screeching and screaming at the top of their lungs as they beat the crap out of a piñata with a baseball bat. The enthusiasm they put it into it would be kinda cute if they hadn't taped pictures of various guys to their target. I don't need to be a genius to figure out those are the exes and the ladies are in a homicidal mood. As I watch, planning my extraction, the piñata gives up the ghost, flying apart at the seams and launching streamers, bits of photos, and candy into orbit. I pick a Snickers off my boot. Free snacks are the best. This is better than a movie.

Is it better than the titty bar however?

A small, curvy bombshell tears after a tall brunette. The tinier chick is bundled in a pair of men's sweatpants and a white wife beater. She could find a job at *Tits Up* easily because she's skipped the bra and she bounces left and right in a spectacular display of cleavage. A flannel shirt hangs off her waist. I've seen Sarah Jo around town a few times and rumor has it she's about to start working at fire camp as a cook, but she's always done an awesome impression of a turtle and practically yanked her head inside her oversized clothes to avoid meeting my gaze. But tonight she's laughing. Fuck me, she's practically cackling as she tackles the taller, yoga-pants-wearing gal and levels her.

I give her props for the take down, but what comes next is even better. Fucking dinner and a show tonight. I rip open the Snickers and lean against a handy tree. Sarah Jo and the other chick both lunge for the same super-sized licorice rope, tussling and laughing. If God were feeling benevolent, this is when the skies would open up and rain down enough water to turn this wrestling match into a mud fight. That would be fucking awesome.

Since the California drought shows no signs of quitting, however, I enjoy what I've got. Sarah Jo is no quitter, but the brunette chick has some crazy talented moves. They roll around, legs going everywhere, asses in the air, and Sarah Jo's wife-beater climbs steadily toward her tits as she battles for control of the licorice rope. Moments later, she springs to her feet, waving the candy over her head. As if that's not enough, she dances away, tears open the plastic wrapper, and licks the red tip.

Fuck. Me.

I need a distraction. I need to grab my boy and get the hell out of here. I do *not* need to start imagining Sarah Jo's mouth closing around my dick and sucking me deep. It doesn't take a genius to figure out that whatever's brought Sarah Jo here to Big Bear Lake, she's got some serious issues and she doesn't want attention. She wears more clothes than a convention of Mormons.

Lola and Hunter are squabbling about something. I take a step closer, trying to ignore the iron bar in my pants. It's like a fucking dowsing rod except it's pointing straight to Sarah Jo. I guess she's a cool drink of water. She's certainly cold enough. Despite being one of Big Bear Lake's few single women, she's made it plenty clear that *dating* and *when hell freezes over* are synonymous in her own personal dictionary. I don't aim my hose where it hasn't been invited, so I focus on Hunter and Lola, who's busy giving him loud crap about his refusal to join in the mad scramble for the piñata's contents. The woman has three volumes: loud, louder, and loudest.

"Who doesn't like candy?" she says, hands on hips.

Hunter opens his mouth to disagree, so I step in

and save his ass. He can thank me later.

"Better listen to your girl."

Both Lola and Hunter turn to stare at me like they're surprised to see me. Do I need an engraved invitation to crash their shenanigans?

"What's up?" Hunter doesn't sound thrilled. He starts patting his pocket as if he's looking for his phone. He probably thinks I've come about a fire instead of on a mission of mercy.

"Came to drag you out with us," I announce.

Did that sound like a threat to you? Because my words definitely get the attention of the two wrestlers. The brunette chick just snorts something under her breath, but Sarah Jo bolts toward us, grabbing the abandoned baseball bat. She goes all watchdog, her fingers tightening on the handle as she raises it like she's more than ready to take a swing at any shit I toss her way. Hunter tenses. Lola mutters something. Hello, DECFON two.

And Sarah Jo stares at me. She's got both hands on the bat. She looks downright terrified. I know I'm a big guy. I came out of the dark with no warning. But when she looks at me, I don't think she sees me at all. She's watching her past or some really bad memories—and she's working herself up to take a swing at those demons.

I step out of the shadows and into the light so she can get a good look at me. She's welcome to hit me if it makes her feel better but I want full credit for any skull-cracking I allow. This also gives me a better view of her face.

I could look at her face for hours. She's pocket-sized compared to my bulk, a tiny, curvy dynamo biting a pair of lush, pink lips. I'd be happy to do the biting for her, to nibble on her all night. Her top slides down one shoulder and I have to force my eyes to stay put and not detour downward with her shirt. I mentioned she wasn't wearing a bra, right? So you should pin a fucking medal on me right now. She'd be fucking hot if she didn't look so scared. I may look like a Neanderthal, but I do have some rules. Consent is one of them. Orgasms and happiness for all is another.

I slide my hands up in the air. "Didn't mean to startle you."

Sarah Jo doesn't say anything—and she doesn't lower the bat. Her breath sort of whistles in and out, like she's this close to losing her shit. I don't know what would happen then, but I do know it wouldn't make her happy. And she looks like the kind of girl who needs and deserves happy. Maybe it's the pink in her hair. It's a fucking cheerful color. It's also still all messed up from her wrestling match, half falling out of the ponytail thing she's pulled it back in, half bouncing around her face.

"Gotcha," she mouths and takes a step backward. She lowers the bat but doesn't let go of it.

"Brought company with me." I nod toward the truck at the bottom of the driveway. If this girl gets any more scared, she might come apart at the seams. Someone picks this moment to open the truck's door, light spilling into the cab. Looks like Adrian's finally woken up and is in search of a tree for a pee break. Awesome. His free-swinging dick can finish the job of terrifying Sarah Jo. While she takes in the truck's occupants, I inventory the surrounding carnage. The body count includes the dead piñata, a shit-ton of candy, and a half-dozen empty ice cream cartons. Clearly, no one here is lactose-intolerant.

"Busy night," I say out loud.

Hunter eyes me. He's given up looking for his phone. "What's up?"

I lift a shoulder and check to make sure Sarah Jo isn't sneaking up on me with her bat. "We're headed to the bar." I lean in and whisper-shout the next part just to give him shit. "The titty bar. You in?"

Hunter grunts less than enthusiastically. "I'm busy."

"I can see that." I smirk. "You and your girl are having one hell of a date night."

Not my business if he wants to ménage a trois it with these ladies, although it's downright selfish to hog all the single ladies. The man should learn to share his toys.

"We're—" Hunter's gaze slides to Lola, dips over her, and then moves on to the other ladies. He looks like he wished the words *titty bar* had never come out of my mouth.

"You're seeing each other." I drop down onto one of the logs by the fire and stretch my legs toward the flames. My seat's not Barcalounger material, but I've parked it on worse out in the field. "You made her a cute little fire of her own and now you're spending quality time together. I get it. Congratulations, man."

Colt chooses this moment to make his grand appearance. Adrian has either gotten lost taking an epic piss or he's crashed in the truck again. He pulled a late shift yesterday and he's punch-drunk tired. He'll be a lot of fun once I get a beer or six into him.

"Our boy coming with?" Colt asks.

I smirk. "Nope. He's got a date with Lola, so we're flying solo tonight."

Colt looks over at Lola and his face lights up, dimples working overtime. It's amazing the guy ever managed to win any races in his former life given how much time he devotes to thinking about girls. "He's dating Lola Miller?"

I think he's gearing up to offer himself as a substitute if Hunter's not, so I jump in. Besides, if we wait for Hunter to find his words, we'll still be here tomorrow. Hunter makes an iceberg look chatty. "Yeah."

"Wow." Colt whistles. "She doesn't seem like his type."

"I know, right?" I lean back. "She's a class four rapid and he's a really deep, really still pool of water."

"Stagnating," Colt adds.

"We're not seeing each other," Hunter protests. The poor sucker might even think he means it.

"Right." My smirk gets deeper. He's deciding where to punch me first. I can tell.

Or maybe he's just coming up with stupid crap to say because the next words out of his mouth are: "Can you imagine anything less likely than Lola and I?"

"Oil and water," Colt grins. "Yeah. We can see that. But sometimes that's fun."

Colt would know. The man's an equal opportunity dater.

"Lola and I are not having fun together," Hunter insists.

And... we have lift off.

Lola raises her phone and snaps a picture of Hunter. "I'm buying a new piñata."

"Not dating, huh?" I knew Hunter was lying.

"No," he snaps.

"You suck," Lola announces. She stomps toward her truck. Colt, being a smart man, hightails it down the driveway to move his own truck out of her way. From the look of extreme displeasure on Lola's face, she'd happily run our ride over if it got in her way.

"Not dating anymore," I say helpfully. "You totally fucked that up."

I finish my Snickers bar while Hunter holds some painful-looking internal debate with himself. I'm not much for monologuing myself.

"You ready to hit *Tits Up*?" I ask more to help him along. The look on his face is downright constipated. Whatever he's contemplating, it's not making him happy. A beer can only help, but he's clearly not open to suggestions at the moment.

Hunter grumps something in my direction that might or might not be words and then strides off. Seconds later I hear the growl of a truck engine.

"Hope to fuck that's not my ride," I say to the rapidly emptying fire circle. I don't think Colt would leave me stranded, but it's been a weird night.

Sarah Jo makes a peeping sound from where she's hovering on the edge of the action. Frankly, I'm surprised she hasn't hightailed it back into the cabins and barricaded her door. Guess she really is hiding a backbone under all those clothes.

"Oscar the Grouch," she says quietly.

"Excuse me?" I give up trying to play it cool so as not to crowd her or scare her. She could have ignored me or slunk away but she stuck around. Now she gets to talk with me. My dick perks right back up.

"That's what everyone calls him, right? He's just acting in character." She shrugs, like it's no big deal. Maybe it isn't. Maybe she's used to polite, gentlemanly, suit-wearing guys and some kind of Zen-like quiet zone shit in her personal life. Maybe that's why I freaked her out so badly, coming out of the dark like a caveman as I did.

I don't want to scare her. I should get up, go, give her her space. Instead, I keep right on talking.

"You gonna hit me with that?" I nod at the bat she's still clutching. The brunette seems to have disappeared, and we're alone with the fire someone needs to put out. Sarah Jo's eyes dip to the bat in her hand. She looks sort of surprised, like she's not sure how she ended up armed and dangerous. I'm sure plenty of criminal careers have started that way.

She mumbles something and tosses the bat onto the ground. Not too far away, I can't help but notice. But then she lays in a course for me and comes right on over. She even offers me a handful of candy. The stuff's probably been on the ground and beaten to a pulp by her bat. Piñatas have never struck me as terribly hygienic, but I snag her offering and tear open a package of mini M&Ms. The fire camp's down a cook—again—and it was slim pickings in the cafeteria earlier tonight. The girls who cook for us can't keep up with the demand. Sarah Jo sinks down on the edge of the log.

Since she looks a little hesitant, I try to be helpful. "I only eat little girls on Wednesdays and Thursdays, so you're safe."

"Until next week." She sighs with mock seriousness. "Duly noted, Mister Hotshot."

"You gonna give me shit if I stay here?" I drag my palm over my head. Fucking need to get a haircut sometime soon or I'll look like Colt with his stupid, stubby man bun.

"You want to hang out here?" She sounds vaguely horrified.

Do I?

"Might be hazardous." I rub my hand over my chin and give her my best mock-thoughtful look. "Seeing as how folks here like to wander around armed and dangerous."

She snorts. *Win.*

Colt picks this minute to prove he's waiting for me after all. The man starts honking up a storm. The cocksucker thinks he's got musical talent because he varies the beeps and lengths like he's playing me a symphony of hurry-the-fuck-ups. I get that sitting around in the dark waiting on my ass isn't his idea of a good time, but I'd like to know that Sarah Jo's okay. That's what you do when you accidentally scare the shit out of someone. On the other hand, if she says she's not fine, I'm not sure what I'll do. Colt won't wait all night for me and the only fix-it solutions I have are duct tape or kissing it better.

But I have to ask. "Are you okay?"

The question has her looking at me like I'm an idiot. "Fine."

I gesture toward the bat. "You sure?"

"Yes." She blows out her breath in a big huff, making her bangs dance around her face. I'm not sure how she got just parts pink, but it's a talent.

"So you're totally, completely good."

She holds up three fingers. "Scout's honor."

And as if that's not bad enough, seeing her tuck her pinky finger into her thumb and make the perfect space for my dick to play slip-and-slide, she sticks her tongue out at me. *Hell yeah*, my dick bellows. My inner caveman demands we toss her over our shoulder and find a mattress stat.

Time to go.

"You're safe up here." I have no idea where the fuck *those* words come from. They sort of slip out and I can practically see them hanging in the air between us. They also translate nicely into *you fucking idiot*. Sarah Jo's fuckhot and more than a little sweet, but she's made her disinterest in me—in *any* part of me, enormous hose included—perfectly clear and I have a hands-off, eyes-only date with a dancer named Candy Jones anyhow.

Sarah Jo blinks at me and chews on her lower lip as she processes my promise. She's got a streak of caramel on her lower lip; she must have stolen the last Twix. I'm not sure how it happens, but my thumb swipes gently at the sticky spot. I'd rather lick her clean—and then lick her dirty for good measure. Too much? Yeah. I think so, too. She's barely met me.

"You want to come with us?" I'm not sure where that idea came from. It's not like there's some kind of hard-and-fast rule that tit owners dance on stage and non-possessors-of-tits cool their junk in the audience, but I can't remember ever seeing a girl watching the show. But maybe Sarah Jo's the kind of person who likes breaking barriers. Maybe watching some girl shake her stuff is exactly what she likes to be doing best.

"To *Tits Up*?" She's not scared anymore. Nope. She's fucking shaking with laughter. Good to know I'm no longer the big, bad wolf.

"We can hit the place up." I grin at her. Fuck, she's kind of fun when she's not hiding in her clothes. "Grab a beer. See the show. My treat."

"Pass." She makes a face. "If I want to see boobs, I

can look down the front of my shirt."

"You could pretend to be disappointed," I point out. "You know, you're rough on a guy's ego. First you scream and point when you see me, and now you won't even let me buy you a beer."

"At a strip club." She gets busy untying her flannel shirt from her waist and covering up. Guess she's definitely remembered that I have a dick.

"Huh." I stand up as Colt lays on the horn again. If he abandons me here, it's a long walk back to fire camp. "Well in the spirit of fairness, we could look at tits tonight and then next weekend we could ride over to Sacramento. Find the Chippendales or something so we can look at dick packages."

And then she giggles. She looks me straight in the eye, her face lights up, and she makes this fantastically dorky, wonderful high-pitched heehaw of sound that's better than a million porn moans of *do me harder, big guy.*

"You have a good night," she says.

I already am.

And that, ladies and gentlemen, is how I met the mother of my children. She didn't know it yet, but Sarah Jo was about to become mine.

2

SARAH JO

"KISS the first hotshot you see. Whoever's first in line, just lay one on him." Rosalie waves her spatula for her emphasis, ponytail bouncing like an exclamation point. She's the head cook at fire camp and my boss for the last few weeks, which means I'm supposed to do what she says. Somehow, I don't think sexually harassing the hotshot firefighters was what HR had in mind.

Another cook mimes kissing, hooking a tanned arm around the neck of an imaginary lover. "A hot kiss, mind you. You're not kissing your grandma. A little lip, a little tongue—that lucky boy won't know what hit him. Nothing to it. And nothing you haven't done before, I bet."

Oooh… now my co-workers are speculating about *my* sex life. So much for my plan to keep a low profile—I'm about as visible now as a fireworks show on top of Mount Kilimanjaro. I stand there staring at them like I've never heard of kissing, tugging my oversized flannel shirt tighter around me. It's big enough that I could use it as a tent. Or a turtle shell. If I were super smart, I'd pull my head inside the flannel and not come out for another century or two.

"A hot kiss for a hotshot," another whoops.

We're an equal opportunity camp: if men think about sex constantly, so do the women. Even me. I devote plenty of mental time to kissing. First kisses, dirty kisses, kisses with tongue, butterfly kisses… don't make me pick between them. I'm an "E—All of the above" woman when it comes to choosing my favorite. Rough kisses, soft pecks, Eskimo kisses, French kisses—yes, yes, and yes please. Really, even bad kisses aren't all bad because you can share a good laugh with your fellow kissee about whatever it is that went wrong.

So other than the sad fact that I need to *not* draw

attention to myself, I don't have any problem with my boss's demand that I kiss a hotshot. I'm happy to take one for the team and add to the photo gallery I'm keeping in my head. You thought only guys stored up spank bank material? Think again. Last night over s'mores and before the piñata-smashing main event, my friend Lola suggested we rename the spank bank.

Rub club.

Jill till.

The flick file.

I've stored up my favorite kisses over the years, and yes, I re-run them in my head when it's time for a little ménage a moi. I may have a kissing addiction, if we're being honest. I've got an entire highlights reel of best-ever kiss moments stored up in my head. I've been accused—with some grounds—of preferring the warm up kisses to the main act. Some people make an entire meal out of appetizers and skip the main course. I'm done apologizing for liking what I like—and so if I prefer tongue action to sausage action, so be it.

At the moment, however, I'm on a kissing hiatus. I may just possibly have kissed the wrong guy a little bit too much, resulting in my presence in this fire camp in Nowheresville, California. A girl has to kiss a lot of frogs to find her prince, and my last frog was a warty one with nary a crown in sight. I got no magic fairy tale ending where he morphed into Mr. Tall, Dark, and Regally Handsome in order to sweep me off my feet in his private Learjet to some obscure but filthy rich European country. I was the happy recipient of no tiara, no happily-ever-after, and no super-talented dick. Instead, I've ended up with life on the lam and a minimum wage job that requires me to both cook *and* do the dishes.

The cafeteria I'm standing in used to be a mess hall back in Civilian Conservation Corps days, a period that I'll put in the category of long, long ago. The building is still largely utilitarian, but the words dilapidated, rundown, and on its last legs also come to mind because the decorating style runs to worn linoleum and fuzzed-out screens. The cooks prop the screen door open with a rock. It definitely isn't the Ritz, with its wooden picnic tables dotting the surrounding clearing for the overflow crowd.

And it's certainly no dating Mecca.

Not that I'm interested in dating.

Or guys.

Sex and anything to do with the penis-possessing

members of society are strictly off-limits, see the aforementioned plan of flying under the radar and sticking to the spank bank. I'm supposed to be hiding, not drawing attention to myself.

"I can't just kiss the first guy I see." My mouth protests, on auto-pilot while my libido considers the option. Seriously. The Big Bear Rogues light fires that have nothing to do with the trees and protecting the wildland interface. I secretly suspect that the nineteen men and one woman (go, sister!) who make up the elite team of wildland firefighters were hired as much for their pretty faces as for their fierce firefighting skills. Or maybe it's the combination of a big, rough lumberjack of a man who's bulked up even more by long weeks hauling a fuck-ton of equipment around the wild. Hell, I'd interface with Pick Revere, one of the hotshot team's two seconds-in-command, any day of the week and twice on Sunday. We've only met once, much earlier in the summer before I started working here, but it was memorable. Even if he did accidentally scare the hell out of me, how do you forget that much man?

Pick is a bear of a man. When cooking gets boring—and since I'm no Michelin chef, I'm usually bored—I amuse myself by imagining him as a frontiersman. My brain likely has too much free time, but I've spent a lot of time lately contemplating the honed muscle and disciplined focus that is Pick. He's precisely the kind of man who knows his way around the forest, and I've invented an entire resume for him. Fantasy Pick is comfortable with a hunting rifle or a ten-mile hike because he's grown up on a diet of outdoor activities. He also moves with an easy confidence that does unspeakable *things* to my insides.

Because you just have to wonder if he knows his way around a bed and a woman's body just as well.

Nope, there's no missing this particular Big Bear Rogue. He loves what he does, showing up for more fires than even Hunter Black does. First in, last out, those two are practically joined at the firefighting hip. Perhaps I should add a ménage a trois to that spank list…

"She's thinking about it," a feminine voice gleefully calls me back to earth.

Snap.

"You don't think an uninvited kiss smacks of"—I wave my spatula for emphasis before prying the slightly charred pancake off the griddle I'm manning—"sexual harassment? Won't I be setting myself up for a sure meet and greet with a pink slip?"

I totally need to hang on to this job. Paychecks don't magically deposit themselves into my checking account. I was down to my last few dollars when I stopped for gas in Big Bear Lake, California and saw the avalanche of Help Wanted and For Rent posters pinned to the wall. Old-fashioned kind of cute, I thought, tickled that someone still went the 8-x-11 route with a strip of tear-off numbers on the bottom.

Since being unemployed and on the run meant that I had time to kill and nowhere to be, I read while I worked my way through a car-warmed Coke. And it's like Karma or God herself tapped on my shoulder because that's how I'd found out about the Break Up Club. Or maybe my attention had been grabbed by the Craigslist posting printed out on hot-pink construction paper decorated with copious swirls of glitter glue. The sign screamed *Look at me!* and practically blinded me when a ray of sun hit the paper. Apparently, I had a once-in-a-lifetime opportunity to join said Break Up Club and "work through" the demise of a recent relationship. The poster promised an eight-step master plan guaranteed to purge douches, exes, and troublesome penes from every area of my life.

Since I didn't want my ex finding me under any circumstances, *purging* sounded right up my alley. Even better? The Break Up Club was a sleepaway camp. Members got dibs on "charmingly rustic" cabins "situated in a pristine mountain environment." I dialed the number pronto and became founding member number three. Finding semi-permanent shelter of the non-car variety had been step one in my Reinvent Sarah Jo plan, and even if I've ended up in a cabin that made tiny living look palatial, I'm happy. I have a roof, running water, and my own bathroom. It's a definite step up from the cardboard box I'd envisioned when I bolted from Auburn. It's possible that situation there could have sorted itself out, but I'll take my chances on the cabin and the hotshots.

Work even magically fell from the sky and landed in my lap. I called on a few of the Help Wanted posters, and thanks to a completely understandable lack of people willing to make millions of pancakes for minimum wage, I ended up here. Thank God no one actually tested my cooking abilities before saying the magic words *you're hired*. With my phone and Google, I can fake anything. I also flipped a digit on my Social—close enough to excuse if and when someone notices—

and gambled no one had time to run a full background check when they were shorthanded. Hotshots can eat their weight in pancakes, I kid you not.

But back to the whole sexually-assault-a-hotshot thing. I'm sure you want to know how that turns out. I know I do.

Rosalie's shaking her head. She's still stuck on the whole kissing thing. "Those boys like a good joke."

"Uh-huh." Frowning, I examine my pancake. One side is definitely edible. The other? Not so much. With a mental shrug, I carefully position the pancake on the stack. Show only the good side. I've learned that, haven't I? Strategic cover-up is the story of my life.

"The first guy in line. That's the dare." Rosalie crosses her arms over her ample chest where large letters declare *Firefighters light me up* and with which statement I am in whole-hearted agreement. It's like mountain scenery. Sometimes, you just have to stop and stare.

"I dare you," she continues. "We all had to do it. You want to be a summer cook and one of us, you kiss the guy."

"I'm hardly new," I point out. "I've been working here for over a month."

Rosalie grins at me. "Yeah, but none of us thought you'd last this long."

She makes a good point.

What she *doesn't* know, however, is that the sad state of my checking account combined with my secret escape plan means that I have plenty of incentive to stick with the job, even if it isn't fantasy fodder material. You know. Except for the sexy hotshots that parade through my line every day.

"I'm a sticker," I say virtuously. It's not like I'm pro-quitting, after all. I can *totally* polish my halo on this one.

"Uh-huh." Rosalie snorts and points at my pancake. The one I've flipped over to hide the burned bits. "Hope you kiss better than you cook."

Rising to the bait is stupid, but I've never liked backing down from a dare. I can do this. I just have to hope that the first man in line is decent looking. Yes, I'm shallow that way, but if I'm getting my first kiss in months, I want a *good* one.

"Hostile work conditions," I grouse, pouring more batter out of the ancient Tupperware container. The griddle spits and hisses, trying to christen my forearms with second-degree burns. My flannel is multipurpose—camouflage *and* protective gear.

"Honey, you want hostile, you go out there." Rosalie jerks a thumb southeast where a thick column of oily black smoke punches up over the horizon. Seen from a distance, the fire is little more than a thick, sluggish haze right now. The hotshots headed out early this morning, on a mission to keep the fire small. Early is the perfect time to catch a fire and put it out. Later, when the sun rises and the day heats up, fire becomes a bear to stop, or so I've learned. I eavesdrop on a lot of conversations while I'm serving pancakes.

"You really did it?" I have to ask.

"Kissed the first man I saw? Honey, you bet I did. That hotshot didn't know what hit him. Took him home with me, too, and kept him." Rosalie laughs, amusement shaking her entire frame.

"This isn't some kind of weird dating service, is it?" My suspicion is a hard-learned lesson. If a perfectly lovely, noble white steed popped its ass onto my front lawn I'd absolutely look it in the mouth. I'd run a background check on it too because no matter how pretty a horse is, it's still going to shit all over your grass and generally make a public nuisance of itself.

Case in point? I went out with a perfectly

respectable deputy sheriff, no questions asked, and *that* ex-boyfriend burned a house down around my ears and blamed me for the ensuing property destruction. To avoid certain legal charges, I've transplanted my city-loving self here to fire camp. Big Bear is my second chance, and sex isn't on my to-do list. Although a kiss hardly counts as sex. A quick peck on the lips, a flirty answer to the girls' dare, and my place here this summer is secured. *Ka-ching.*

The other cooks already have questions. Fitting in usually isn't a problem for me even if irreverent is my middle name and I'm never quite certain when to shut my mouth and when to let her rip. But most people like a good laugh and I enjoy the company. Based on the super charred state of the pancake in my frying pan, however, I've still got fitting-in issues to resolve.

The noise of the returning crew drowns out Rosalie's laughter. Battered pickups bounce over the rutted road, disgorging a load of hot, sweaty, buff hotshots and the unmistakable smell of smoke, outdoors, and something else indefinably masculine. If I could bottle the *eau de hotshot*, I'd never need to flip another pancake because I'd be a billionaire with a private island in Fiji.

The horde approaches. It's refreshing that they eye my food and not my boobs.

One kiss. How can it hurt? I can go back to hiding in plain sight afterward.

"I'm in."

Rosalie tosses me a pot of cherry lip gloss. "Lube it up, honey. Give him something to remember."

PICK

It's amazing how much suckage can be packed into twenty-four hours and mine have been a fucking overachiever starting with the crap roads. Part fire access, part logging route, the pavement ran out after twenty yards, forcing me to bump northwest for hours. The ruts were deep enough that I fucking feared for my balls each time my truck bottomed out. Then, the pumper truck had hit mud left over from last week's storm and bogged down. The boys and I had thrown a cable around a handy tree and winched like hell trying to pull the truck out. Eventually, I'd had to dump almost two hundred gallons of water to lighten the load.

Which totally worked.

Until the next colossal mud puddle did the truck in again. It was like being stuck in the Groundhog Day movie, re-living the same crappy moments over and over. God was probably laughing his ass off at the outtakes too. Me and him need to sit down and discuss all the ways he's decided to keep my ego in check, preferably over a cold beer. I think we could come to some kind of amicable arrangement.

The fire hadn't cooperated, either. Eventually, after an all-night battle with the wind picking up and fanning the flames for a steep upslope run, we'd been forced to admit that fire was now burning out of control and hand tools wouldn't get the job done. We'd called for a tanker drop, packed up our shit, and started the long drive back to camp. Lining up for pancakes and coffee seems like a waste of time when there's still fire to fight, but fresh guys are manning the line now and the higher-ups have decided that the Rogues need the rest. The sooner we start on the downtime, the sooner we can head back out there. Plus, God owes me that beer and I intend to collect.

I park my truck on auto-pilot, replaying the last

hours in the field in my head. Some guys like their sports highlights or porn stars, but usually it's just me and fire in my head. Take that line ten feet farther south and call in the tanker twenty minutes sooner . . . That right there was where the day had gone FUBAR. That's fucked up beyond all recognition for you sensitive flowers who never have to put a quarter in the swear jar. A hand slaps me on the back, jolting me out of the full-color replay in my head.

The hand belongs to Hunter Black and is quickly retracted. He doesn't look much happier to be on recall, either, but at least he's got a girl. Maybe. Possibly. He's been doing a kind of complicated dating/mating dance with one Lola Miller. They're not officially a couple, but they're definitely friends with benefits, as her rampaging on Piñata Night seems to imply. She's hot as fuck, more colorful than a rainbow, and an aspiring actress who somehow manages to turn every encounter into a dramatic scene. Hunter is usually our resident Oscar the Grouch, but ever since he and Lola started shaking the sheets or hanging together, he's practically been Suzy Fucking Sunshine. Right now, however, the look on his face is less than pleasant, so I'm betting he's thinking about our fire instead of his maybe girl.

Hunter doesn't bother with pleasantries as he falls into step beside me. There's no need to say *hi* and *bye* given the quality time we spend together. "Not ready to pack it in?"

I snort and move forward with a groan as every muscle in my body protests. Too bad the fire camp hasn't invested in masseuses. Or masseuse-strippers. Who serve filet fucking mignon and ice cold beers. I take a moment to appreciate that little fantasy. Ever since I got a little banged up and singed earlier this summer, I've been noticing the aches and pains more often. It's like my body's been put on high alert and wants to make sure I don't inflict any more grievous bodily harm on my various limbs. What the hell is wrong with me?

"Not likely. You?"

"Nope," Hunter replies. He's a man of few words. There's a reason why he's been compared to Oscar the Grouch—and why Oscar has always come out ahead in any contest of manners. "And yet here we are. Back in base camp."

The benching of our asses is a temporary state of affairs, I remind myself. Tomorrow's another day. Blah fucking blah. Insert your platitude here, but I guarantee one thing. I *will* be out there, and I will be fighting fire.

Hunter stares balefully at the plume blocking out the daylight. He's also thinking what I'm thinking. "Plenty of fire out there to go around. She'll still be there when we finish our R and R."

A couple of the guys bypass us, double-timing it toward their trucks. Must have a hot date in town. I can't remember the last time I pulled that kind of shit myself, but I'm not a flower and roses guy. You want sex, I'm happy to put out. I'll bring you to heaven and back and make you come so hard that you see stars, but I'm not gonna open doors or make restaurant reservations. I won't remember to call, I don't do anniversaries, and I don't care if you went to the trouble to pick out a matching panty and bra set. I just want you naked, wet, and willing.

Hunter, however, is well on his way to being officially pussy-whipped thanks to Lola. I don't know if she's just got a magic pussy or he's let her hijack his heart, but I don't want that. Why would I? Relationships require work, and I've already got a full-time job. Hunter fishes his phone out of his pocket, spends a long moment searching for cell service, and then proceeds to thumb through about forty million texts from his female overlord. From the dazed look on his face, I'm pretty sure Lola sent him a naked selfie. I'm just not gonna ask of what—Lola's good people but she's not shy. I don't need to accidentally spot her beaver shot.

Does it sound like I'm not happy for Hunter? Because I totally am. It's just part of the man code that I have to give him shit because he's getting regular sex in exchange for letting Lola housebreak him. The rest of the team already has a betting pool going on whether or not he pops The Question before fire season ends. The odds are split pretty evenly at the moment between Hunter investing in some high-quality diamonds and Hunter running for the hills. He's already got one bad marriage under his belt, so I placed my ten bucks on his splitting. In the meantime, however, he's spending time with her like the sex shop is about to close up and he needs to make his purchases now, now, now.

I don't have the same draw to leave camp. In all honesty, I don't have much of a home to go back to. That makes a difference. If you've got the Four Seasons and limitless kinky sex waiting for you, you're gonna haul ass, right? My life is more like the Motel 6 with the vibrating bed that you feed quarters into—and that craps out on you mid-thrust.

The fire camp is a temporary way station. Like many of the guys, I've got my RV and my pillow, but where I hit the hay doesn't matter much. Sure, sleep sounds good right now, as does a real hot shower, but getting my hands on a Pulaski and digging line sounds better. I like to finish what I start, whether that's in bed or in the forest. It's my job to kick fire's ass, and the higher ups in the forest service had decided I wasn't going to get the chance today.

"We were close," I growl when Hunter finally looks up from the picture he's salivating over. "Another hour and we'd have had her."

Leaving a problem unfixed goes against the grain. Fixing what's wrong just makes sense. Eight hours of knocking down flames, shoveling dirt wherever the orange pops up. Everything is dry and heated, ready to go up at a moment's notice, and then the wind shifts and we're suddenly staring defeat in the face. The flames had hopped the line we'd scratched out like all our work was nothing and raced upslope. Fire doesn't offer do-overs. Just overtime.

"Maybe." Hunter shrugs and pockets his phone. "But rules are rules, and coming in for a few hours isn't hurting us."

"You say that because you've got a date with Lola tonight." Hunter's fascination with the actress is an unending source of amusement for our team, and the guys miss no chance to give Hunter guff. When we'd found out about her national laundry detergent commercial, we'd packed Hunter's bed full of the big, blue containers. "You taking her somewhere good this time?"

Hunter's romantic repertoire makes me look like the world's most talented Don Juan.

"I've got plans." Hunter grins.

No, no, no.

Change the topic. Do *not* imagine what's on his to-do list for tonight. I eyeball the chow line, instead.

"We're first in line." I'm never first. Don't get me wrong—it's not because I'm gonna voluntarily hang back and let someone else charge the goodies. The breakfast line is usually more stampede than orderly queue, and my teammates play dirty. It's weird, because while we're not Miss Fucking Manners, out in the field we look out for each other like we're channeling our inner Musketeers and it's one for all and all for one no matter how much fire Mother Nature tosses at us. Add pancakes to that equation, however, and I'm surprised we still have twenty hotshots. Pretty sure that if we were in a plane that crashed in the middle of the Himalayas, none of us would hesitate to eat the others. Tastes like chicken, right?

Hunter looks at me and I give him a big ass grin. It never hurts to play nice. Hunter's gaze narrows as he takes in the cooks, waiting to serve up the day's breakfast, and then he shoves me forward. "After you."

I smell pancakes, bacon, and nothing out of the ordinary. "Not hungry?"

"Not for what those girls are cooking up." He backs up, putting some more space between me and him.

Danger.

I eyeball the row of stainless steel heating trays. Still looks like pancakes and bacon to me. Smells like breakfast with a side of Styrofoam and coffee. Whatever trouble he sees, I'm not seeing—and I'm hungry as fuck. I look behind me, and sure enough, the rest of the team is hanging back. What's up with that? It's not my birthday and I'm not *that* much older than the other guys even if they do like to call me *Gramps.* Or *Grumps.* Age before beauty, right? Looks like I'm taking one for the team.

"Avenge my death," I mock-whisper to Hunter and

slap him on the back even harder than he walloped me in the spirit of keeping things even.

By the time I reach the start of the food line, I've figured a few things out. My teammates may have cleared the way to the pancakes for me like Moses parting the Red Sea, but looks like it's a one-man pass. As soon as I've gone, they all fall in behind me, jostling for position like they always do. Whatever's up, it's only gonna shit on me and that's fine because I've just spotted an unexpected bright spot in an otherwise suck-ass day.

Sarah Jo is working the line today.

Her haphazardly buttoned flannel shirt gapes as she shovels pancakes into a stainless steel warmer, giving me an excellent view of her blue T-shirt that announces *Firemen do it hotter*, the pink curlicues scrolling across her tits. I know she's wearing the matching hot-pink bra because the lacy strap peeking out from beneath its evil cotton overlord just screams *look at me*. So I do. Even though I shouldn't. It's like being handed a beer when you've decided tonight is a dry night or a slab of chocolate cake an hour after you start that diet. I have no will power when it comes to Sarah Jo, just a whole lot of dirty thoughts, and I'd absolutely love to show her how *this* fireman does it.

The truth is, I am dirty. Whether she is is still up for debate. The last time I saw her, she was more scared than turned on. I remind myself that makes her *really* off-limits while I grab a plate and a napkin full of rolled up silverware. She's wearing my favorite skirt, too, the one made out of some kind of clingy fabric that hugs her ass and stops two inches below the flannel shirt and far, far above her hiking boots. I suspect she thinks wrapping herself up in an acre of used flannel will be some kind of penis deterrent. My dick, however, just decides that she's gift-wrapped herself for us and we should tear into her one button at a time.

My dick has the best ideas.

She glances toward the start of the line, and the southern parts of me perk up and wave hello.

Bad hotshot.

Dating anyone in camp is a potentially messy mistake, and she's given me no real reason to think she might be interested anyhow. Plus, the odds of her lasting the summer are low. She can't cook worth a damn, although her enthusiasm more than makes up for it as far as I'm concerned. Burnt eggs taste way better after I've brushed up against her. Or snuck a peek down the front of her T-shirt when she bends over, flashing me the sweet valley between her tits. Or... yeah. I've got a fucking catalog of dirty fantasies and she's got... coffee. She beams like a lighthouse as she hands out the Styrofoam cups and fusses over her basket of Mini Moos and sugar. She always remembers how I like mine and hoards the French vanilla creamers for me. Mentally, I smack myself. This sounds way too kindergarten. Maybe I should pass her a note. I could itemize all the ways I like her—and want to do her.

Unlike her ignore-me flannel shirt, her hair demands a second look or three. I still can't decide what the color was. Her chunky strands are a L'Oreal rainbow, browns and blonds mixed up with the occasional streak of red. I've spotted pink, blue, and purple, too. Like her choice of hair color, every emotion she feels is painted on her face. Watching her talk up the other cooks is like staring at a merry-go-round. She's fucking full of life and color, and damned if she doesn't make me dizzy. The ride would be worth it, though.

Yes, I've imagined *riding* her. More than once.

I'm a fucking HR lawsuit waiting to happen, but the truth is what it is and that T-shirt of hers isn't helping any. She looks away, bending over to grab something, and the cotton stretches tight over her breasts, gifting me with another flash of pink and lace. *Black* lace. Christ. Wonder if the boys would be up for a panty raid tonight?

She looks back, and this time her gaze hones in on me like a bird dog sighting quail and her blue-gray eyes light up. Of course, knowing what color her eyes are is just one more sign I'm in trouble.

"Pick Revere," she announces loudly, nodding her head like she's continuing a conversation with herself. Not like I can disagree with my name, so I just let her continue while I grab a plastic tray from the closest stack. "You're first in line. That's just perfect."

Whatever.

In addition to being almost a co-worker, she's too young for me. The first day I laid eyes on her, slinging eggs and hash browns, I'd started running numbers in my head, guessing at her age. I'd pegged her for maybe twenty-four, and I'd last seen that side of thirty more than two years ago. She's part-Goth, part sass—but I'm betting that, beneath the oversized clothes and the skittish demeanor, she's one hundred percent sweet, hot female. She damned certain deserves better than me, and no way she belongs out here in the woods.

I don't even care how she got hired on despite not

being able to cook. Frankly, there aren't too many people interested in camping for the summer, slinging eggs and burgers twelve hours a day for minimum wage. She looks more Corvette or racing car than RV, but she gives her job her all and I respect that.

"Morning." Nodding my head toward her, I heft my tray and eye the dishes on offer. Yep. Pancakes. Bacon. And... beans. I'll pass on those, but otherwise I'll take everything else she has to offer.

"That's settled," she announces. I think about that for a moment, but I've got nothing. It's like I've just barged in on a half-done conversation.

She steps around the food-laden table and stalks toward me, a determined look in her eye. I've seen fire start up a hill that way, unstoppable and devouring everything in its path. That look spells trouble. I back my ass up, doing a little fancy footwork. What. The . . .

Heaven.

Sarah Jo throws her arms around my neck, stretching up on tiptoe. Her enthusiastic embrace slams the empty tray between us, a plastic chastity belt squashing the fuck out of my balls. I'll catch hell from the boys for that later, but right now all I feel is cheated with that hard plastic pressed against me instead of

Sarah Jo. Those millimeters separating me from her are a fucking shame. She smells good, too. Pancakes and syrup, with a hint of something floral and feminine. She definitely smells better than I do.

She's impatient too, pulling my head down toward her. There's nothing tentative or shy about her, just all that happy laughter filling her eyes and her voice. "It's going to be a real good morning, hotshot."

I open my mouth. Damned if I know what I intend to say, but she takes full advantage. *Hello.*

Her mouth covers mine and she plants a hot kiss on me. Her tongue tastes my bottom lip, sweeps inside, and proceeds to pillage my mouth ruthlessly. When she comes out of hiding, she does it with a vengeance.

The groan escapes before I can bite back the rough, hungry sound. I haven't kissed a woman in a long time. Too many fires, not enough time. My dick likes to argue about my priorities, but I think protecting people's homes from burning up beats anything. Sarah Jo has no idea just how *hungry* I am, or that my inner pirate demands we make a sensual feast out of her body. If she did, she'd run like hell.

But she doesn't know, and she doesn't run. Her mouth locks on mine, her tongue retreating to tease my lower lip with a light stroke that's nowhere near enough. And Christ, when her fingers seek the back of my neck, tracing a little up and down pattern across my bare skin, it's game over.

Being kissed by Sarah Jo is so much better than anything I've imagined—and I have a great imagination. While her tongue explores my mouth with the enthusiasm of an orchestra racing toward the crescendo of a really awesome symphony, I kiss her back as much as she allows. I'm not just gonna be the audience on this kiss—after all, we've already got one. I'm dimly aware of raucous background noise as my fellow Rogues whoop and holler. Pretty sure even the kitchen staff is getting into it, laughing and waving the verbal pom-poms for us. As if I could stop this kiss. As if I'd want to. Mostly, though, I'm aware of the woman in my arms and the sweet scent of her pressed against me. Whether it's shampoo or perfume, or some secret female thing, she smells damned good.

When she pulls back, her lips pink and swollen, and tries to dance away from me, I hold on tight. That mischievous smile of hers tugs at the corner of her mouth.

Too bad for her I'm not done with her yet.

Tossing the tray away, I scoop her closer with one arm. "Honey, I'm definitely wanting seconds today."

SARAH JO

PICK THREADS big hands through my hair, holding me in place for his next kiss. He's either forgotten about or doesn't mind our avid audience, because his mouth covers mine in a take-no-prisoners kiss. He pulls me into his body, a body that's every bit as hard and muscled as I've fantasized—and I've done more fantasizing than is good for me. It's hard not to notice how strong Pick is, from the muscled forearms I'm clutching like a sexual lifeline to the way his shoulders stretch the cotton of his T-shirt. Everything about him shouts that he's got your back, that you're safe from everything and everyone. My inner cave girl squees with delight—she's not totally on board with my *no man—stand on my own feet* plan.

When Pick kisses me again, the rest of me rejects the plan, too. God, he's gorgeous. He's got brown hair that's just long enough for me to run my fingers through, but not quite long enough to hold onto. Pick's the kind of fantasy man who slips through your life, your arms, your dreams. But the way he grins… his whole smile lights up his face and you just have to like him. He's built like an ox—or a stallion. A really big, really hung stallion. This man is Grade A, panty-melting male.

The firm press of his lips follows that full-body caress and then his teeth nip my lower lip with a sweetly erotic sting. When I gasp, he sweeps inside like he belongs there and he's just been waiting for me to open up and hang out the welcome sign.

The whole gosh-darn fire camp could burn down around us now. I don't care—screw fire safety. I want more of *this*. More Pick. More kissing. As first kisses go, this one is amazing and it's going to be the crown jewel of my collection. His tongue strokes mine, mapping my mouth with slow, deliberate thoroughness and leaving behind a wicked burn of pleasure. Hell, the man kisses as if he's the one in charge, and the heated arousal building low in my belly warns me that my body, at least, has zero complaints about the change in management because Pick is one hell of a kisser. Sliding my hands up over his arms, I hang on to his broad shoulders like some kind of sex-crazed kudzu vine as he deepens the kiss further.

This attraction exploding between us is a five-alarm blaze. Pick doesn't pull his punches—he just goes all out as he devours the mouth I've offered him in lieu of pancakes. I've tossed a lit match into dry grass, and now we're both on fire. His mouth moves expertly over mine as he plays a game of show-and-tell about how he's feeling. Hungry. *Possessive*.

Unlike my city dates, who sport expensive colognes, Pick smells of smoke and pine, a woodsy, outdoor scent as wild and rugged as the man himself. He's every lumberjack fantasy come to life, and he needs his very own warning label: *smoking hot fireman... danger of smoke inhalation*. Because when I breathe in, he just works his way deeper inside me. He's big, he's rough, and yet he's impossibly careful in the way he holds me. This is no he-man clinch. I'm not bent over backward like a movie poster heroine. He wraps his enormous arms around me and holds me close while his mouth works wicked, dirty magic on the rest of me. The chest beneath his ash-smudged white T-shirt is as hard and unyielding as the muscled thighs pressed against mine, but I've already figured out for myself that there's not an ounce of give in Pick.

But I'm not supposed to kiss him for real. This is just a hazing rite, a ritual so I can be one of the girls and hide in plain sight just a little more thoroughly. I'm the cook. He's the firefighter. The only thing we have together should be pancakes—not the extremely thick, most impressive dick that makes its presence known when he tugs the plastic lunch tray from between us and tosses it somewhere. Away. If only his clothes would follow.

Pick's big, protective, determined, and rough around the edges. So damn sexy. And for the cherry on my hotshot sundae, he's out there fighting fires to protect homes and lives. That's hero material right there.

The problem is, I've dated heroes before. Sometimes, heroes aren't all that heroic when they get you alone and the capes come off. And I'm not precisely heroine material, either. Why would anyone want to rescue me? And why would I let them? This time, when I pull back, he lets me. And we both know it's *let.* My girl parts sigh in happy protest because they're really, really enjoying his alpha male lumberjack highhandedness even if my head's shrieking *danger danger*.

Chocolate eyes stare at me, probably making connections I don't need him to make because Pick's as smart as he is pretty. Looking at him makes me want to do stupid things, like throw myself at him again, or maybe that's just the rich, warm brown of his steady gaze making me want to lick him. Everywhere.

Pick regards me for another way-too-long minute. I'm not sure what he sees, but he slowly untangles his fingers from my hair. As he steps back with a polite nod of his head and a "Thank you, darling," whoops and catcalls erupt from the hotshots watching the Pick and Sarah Jo Show. Our audience is clearly jonesing for a sequel.

Is that what I want?

He took charge of our kiss and then he just plain took over. So letting him know that he's shaken me—*woken* me—to my very core isn't an option. I'll never let him know how close I came to losing control. Men like Pick don't just take an inch. They take the whole goddamned mile and then some. Putting him in his place suddenly matters a great deal. He's turned the tables on me and I need to turn them back. Fast.

I saunter back to the laughing, clapping cooks.

Game. On.

PICK

IT TAKES twenty-four hours for me to get Hunter alone. The four-thousand acre fire blowing up the side of the nearby mountain is partially to blame for the delay. The blaze starts out small enough. The Rogues arrive and scratch out a line, shoveling dirt over the smoldering embers. But as the day goes on, more grass burns and the fire gets happier, although no trees catch. Right about dinnertime, however, Mother Nature picks a side, the wind kicks up, and we end up with flames crossing the line. The scene explodes, flames devouring the dry grasses and rushing upslope. Boxed in by cliffs, the fire's crackle is overly loud, amplified by the rock walls. The tall, black column punching up into the sky guarantees that every breath I take is thick with smoke and the unmistakable smell of burning. Eventually, the fire's head hits rocks upstream and dies, a lucky break, leaving only the treetops flaming, along with patches of smoldering grass.

Now, fighting fire becomes a routine mop-up followed by a quick break while we wait for the helicopter to swing by and lift us out and back to base camp before it gets too dark to fly. My teammates pass the time by giving me shit about my having been on the breakfast menu yesterday. Several produce videos shot on their phones, and I'm pretty certain we're now Facebook stars. I take a bow, pretending that Sarah Jo's kiss is just a prank. A funny stunt that means nothing.

Maybe it doesn't.

Maybe I'm crazy for thinking that kiss came with possibilities.

I definitely understand the value of a good joke. I get that the camp cooks were teasing Sarah Jo and that I'd been a convenient bystander with a penis and a set of lips to kiss. Any other summer, any other woman, and I'd laugh it off right along with them. I'm not claiming to have fallen in love on the spot. Nope. Not claiming that at all. It's just that I felt something when Sarah Jo kissed me, and I'm almost certain she felt that *something* right back. Maybe I believe in insta-lust. Or sex-ever-after.

Even if I'm not supposed to.

I don't need the HR lecture to know that shaking the sheets with a co-worker is a dumbass move. After the orgasm, I still have to work with her—and she has to work with me. It'll suck if having seen each other naked becomes an issue instead of spank bank material. Ergo, I steer clear of my co-workers, and that includes the camp staff. So it's just too damned bad that Sarah Jo kissed me, because she put ideas in my head and now I'm curious.

Beside me, Hunter's Pulaski chews through the iron-hard ground. Two regulation inches down and then straight back up, turning over the dirt nice and neat. Too bad it isn't as easy to get a handle on Sarah Jo.

I give Hunter side eye, not breaking my own rhythm. Hunter's all muscle and he can keep pace no matter how fast I dig. The front line is loud. Men shout over the roar of chain saws, almost drowned out by the crackle of the fire and the steady chop of the helo ferrying new crew in.

Too tired to bother with subtleties, I open with the truth. "You set me up."

"That kiss?"

I shoot him a look and Hunter just grins. "Uh-huh."

Hunter flips the Pulaski, dropping the hoe end down into the dirt and spreading it around. The line is good. The trees, however, are still a damned problem.

"Hazard tree," I say, jerking my head toward the nearest snag. "She's leaning and the fire's got her good."

Hunter tilts his head back and gives the tree a onceover. He comes to the same conclusion as me. "Let's drop her."

A quick round-trip to the pickup and he returns with a chain saw, the rest of the hotshots falling back to a safe distance.

I fall into step with him as we case the tree. It's a big, gnarly motherfucker, slanting worse than the Tower of Pisa. The risk isn't unacceptable, however, and we've got the team cleared out. Better to drop her safely before her top snaps off and lands on someone's head. Good men die that way every year.

Hunter starts checking the chainsaw while he picks up our previous conversation. "Rumor has it those girls do that every year. It's just a game to them."

Yeah. That secret, unreasonable disappointment comes right back. Sarah Jo kissed me like she meant it. Had she? Or was it all just the game Hunter mentioned? She's got a playful streak if the color in her hair and her T-shirt collection is any indication, but now that I've had a taste of her, I want more.

Lots more.

If she's playing games, I'll play. I totally rock at games. I'll be in it to win it.

I smile. "She distracted me."

Hunter grunts something unintelligible. I don't think it's encouragement.

"Have I ever told you how much I love games? I'm a huge fucking fan." I pin my eyes on the snag, ready to call any movement. Doesn't matter how dirty my plans are for Sarah Jo if my dick gets squashed by a falling tree. Since Hunter's got a girl, I'm assuming he's similarly attached to his equipment.

"Right." Hunter yanks the cord and the chain saw roars to life. "More like you saw Sarah Jo standing there and you lit up like a Christmas tree."

"Did not."

Hunter shakes his head, making the first cut through the trunk. "Say what you want, but if I'd gone first, Lola would have killed me. Those girls are friends."

"Maybe." Lola's definitely a firecracker—the kind with a really short fuse and an endless number of explosions. She's all color and pinwheeling shit that lights everything up while you knock back a beer and try to figure out if it's a dragon or a comet or cosmic poop up there in the sky. I consider pointing this out to Hunter but he's already started on his second cut and he might be tempted to use the saw on me instead. He's super touchy about any implied criticism of Lola.

Do you think she would have gone off on him if her own girlfriend had done the kissing? It's hard to pass that kind of liplock off as an accident. You don't just slip and shove your tongue into some random guy's mouth. Still, Lola's got a great sense of humor. She's also not afraid to use her own mouth. I'm betting she'd either do a whole lot of yelling at Sarah Jo or simply kiss Hunter long enough that he forgot all about an unexpected liplock.

"You liked kissing Sarah Jo," Hunter says. Okay. He fucking bellows it loud enough to be heard two states away because the chain saw's not shy about making noise. The blades roar through the back-cut, and the snag topples. For a long moment, the charred treetop hangs there in the smoky air, undecided which way to fall.

Hunter makes a give-it-up gesture at me. See that look of glee on his face? The way his eyes light up and the corners of his mouth quirk? The bastard got an eyeful when Sarah Jo kissed me, and now he thinks he's getting details. Which he'll then share with Lola, who will turn around and unload on Sarah Jo. Do I look stupid?

I smile. "Watch the sky, hotshot. You're not getting me to kiss and tell."

Calling a warning, I step back. Right on target, the snag comes down in a slow-motion, flaming arc. The clearing lights up like a birthday cake for an octogenarian.

Hunter Black is no talker, either. He's the one who first made friends with the bunch of women who'd rented out a string of cabins ignominiously called *Baby Bears Lodge.* If you're going to name your place after wildlife, you should at least aim for the top of the food chain. Pick a badass predator—not something cute and fuzzy. However bad the name was, however, the cabins are now well-stocked with hot, lonely chicks hosting some kind of summer camp for adults. Hunter confided once that the girls called themselves the Break Up Club and that they were working through the end of their most recent relationships. Since club meetings seem to involve pajamas and ice cream, I can understand why Hunter chooses to stick around. Hell, if they add naked pillow fights to the agenda, I'd join.

Although, on second thought, that might be more of Hunter than I need to see.

Hunter, of course, seems perfectly happy that his days are seemingly numbered. "So was that kiss a onetime thing?"

Let's pause that line of questioning, okay? Anytime someone starts questioning the future of a relationship, it's quitting time. Time to hit the road, to get the fuck out of Dodge before things get even stickier. Sarah Jo kissed me. And she didn't protest when I kissed her back, did she? I'm thinking that if the movie preview is that awesome, I'd be crazy not to see the whole show. Still, I go with the safe answer.

"Sarah Jo's the boss." I'm no prize. Hell, I'm working-class all the way. In the off-season, I own my own garage where I work as a mechanic. I pay my bills, but I'll never be a California billionaire. I'll never wear a suit. I like Budweiser, Monday Night Football, and burgers. That doesn't mean I won't try other things—when I look at Sarah Jo, I can imagine all *kinds* of things I'd like to try on her—but I prefer my shit simple and straightforward. Sarah Jo is going to be complicated as fuck. If I'm a straight line about sex and relationships, she's some multivariate calculus—in Mandarin.

She kissed me—and then she let go so fast I still have whiplash. She peeled that pretty mouth of hers off mine and then she'd danced back behind the serving table. As the guys had jostled forward, elbowing me, I'd stared at her like an idiot. *Thanks*, she'd said, like I was just the Mr. Helpful who'd popped a lid on a jar or passed the salt.

Thanks doesn't begin to cover that kiss. My dick is still singing Hosannas, my fingers itching to find her waist again. Yet she wants to pretend that nothing happened.

Hell, I'd half-expected her to call *next,* and I still don't know what I'd have done then.

Because I'm going to be her next and her last, at least as far as this summer goes.

5

SARAH JO

THE DOOR to my eensy-weensy, closet-sized cabin shudders, waking me from a deep sleep and a very nice dream about a Prince Charming with a shoe fetish. The sound of determined pounding fills my ears, and taking the hint, I bolt off the lumpy mattress and grab my go-bag. Which is really just an extra-large tote with all of my essentials and some clean underwear, but I've prepared. I haven't quite managed to diet down to a size that will fit out the bathroom window easily, but I'm banking on desperation adding oomph to my wriggle.

The door shakes beneath the force of a new blow. Shit. I'm busted, bagged, and nailed. Okay. Not nailed, although my dreamy Prince Charming was about to give it to me good. *Focus.*

I stumble toward the bathroom, clutching my getaway goods. I have to pee, I have to run, I have to…

"Emergency intervention!" Lola bellows from outside. Lola is a stage actress and a drama teacher, so her voice carries effortlessly through my locked door. My sleep-deprived brain is still a few pages behind in the script, so I need a moment to process the words. I haven't been found. Everything's fine, or as fine as it gets when you're on the run and nearly broke and the big, bad wolf's going to bite your butt any day now. Sometimes I think it would be easier to just sit down and wait. Screw the sick anticipation, right?

"Be right there," I croak out. I've spent the last few months trying *not* to be noticed, so I have to repeat myself—twice—before Lola hears me. At least she stops knocking and goes away, although I know she'll be back if I don't make an appearance.

I shove my go-bag/purse back under the bed, grab a sweatshirt, and stagger out. It's approximately dark o'clock, the sky a dense black like a squid pooped ink all over the stars. The late hour doesn't seem to faze Lola, who's now plopped cross-legged in front of our sleek new fire pit.

I'm pretty sure the fire pit is courtesy of Hunter. It showed up one morning shortly after he yelled at us for illegal, unsafe burns in the previous fire pit (which was either a hollowed out, ashy depression in the ground or a metal trash can, depending on our mood and needs). I like Hunter. He's like a loaner brother, big, grumpy, and protective. I'm not sure what's going on between him and Lola, but it guarantees he has zero sexual interest in me, so I can just admire his very manly scenery. Plus, since he's the local Oscar the Grouch, he's not big on conversation, which guarantees that my secrets stay safe.

Lola huffs out a breath as she stares up at me. "Were you asleep? Or engaged in 'personal business'?"

"Huh?" I shouldn't have taken that Melatonin to help me sleep because it's short-circuited a significant number of brain cells. My tongue is thick and my mouth more parched than the Gobi Desert.

Lola tugs me down beside her. One of the drawbacks to our super-cheap cabin-in-the-woods lodgings is that outdoor seating is extremely minimalistic. In other words, we're sitting on logs a previous tenant scavenged from said woods. I try not to think about carpenter ants, termites, or any eight-legged friends that could be trying to get into my pants. Yippee. That's the closest I've been to any non-solo panty action in months.

"Mas-tur-ba-tion," Lola mouths slowly—and at full volume.

Olivia, the third member of our club, raises a brow as she drops a pillow onto the log next to us before sitting down like it's a freaking throne and she's Queen Olivia. She's been sketchy on the details of her qualifying break up, and I don't think that's due to her being shy or private. "Are we planning on a group orgy?"

"Shouldn't we wait for Hunter?" He's the fourth and newest member of the Break Up Club, although by rights we should have denied him membership. He has a penis and this was a girls-only club. As Olivia pointed out, however, discrimination is never okay, so we let him in because his break up story is pretty darn dismal.

Lola cackles. Right. I guess "group orgy" and "wait for Hunter" shouldn't be uttered in close proximity. I give her the finger and wait. Lola doesn't do silence well, which is one of the things I love about her. She's loud, she's colorful, and around her I usually forget the shit that's bothering me.

I'm about to clarify my anti-orgy stance when something rustles in the trees. The problem with Baby Bear Lodge is that it's approximately in the middle of nowhere—a nowhere surrounded by an insane number of trees. During the daylight hours, I don't mind all the vegetation. At the very least, I can pretend I'm starring in my very own version of *Heidi* and that there's nothing more menacing than a bunch of goats nearby. At night, however, it's dark.

Super, super dark.

So I find the stick-cracking noise issuing from somewhere near a gigantic pine tree disturbing. I bolt to my feet. It could be bears. Or killer possums. Or the Douche. Frankly, stalking me in the dark is exactly what the Douche would do. He swore he'd come after me, and I'm sure he's doing exactly that. It's why I've made it my mission to avoid his capturing me. One step ahead. That's all I have to stay.

Another unidentifiable noise emanates from the shadows.

I grab the baseball bat I keep stashed behind the log for midnight defensive maneuvers. I have another one in my cabin because I don't trust myself not to forget it and a girl needs to be armed and dangerous in this world. Olivia bolts to her feet too, but she calmly sweeps the clearing with her eyes. I guess she's looking for whatever shit's about to storm toward us. Her whole body's relaxed, but she looks ready to rumble. I always knew she was a bad ass.

"Stand down." Lola tugs on the hem of my shirt. "Cute wildlife alert."

Sure enough, a raccoon waddles out of the dark, blinks at us, and then scoots down the driveway. Presumably, it's on its way to the dumpster down by the road for a little midnight snackage. Olivia sits back down like it's NBD. Lola starts laughing.

"Are you okay?" Olivia's still got her super calm gaze trained on me.

"I'm fine." I wave my hands like a little breeze might distract them from the way I'm sort of, almost hyperventilating.

Lola rubs my back in little circles. "What are you afraid of?"

It would be stupid to tell her. It—

Olivia throws up a staying hand. "Don't self-incriminate."

When we both turn to look at her, she shrugs. "We've all got secrets," she says.

"Are you holding out on us?" Lola frowns mock-ferociously.

Olivia draws her fingers away from her eyes in a vee. "Don't make me threaten you."

"Oh." Lola chews on that for a moment. A very *short* moment. Then she shrugs and stabs a finger at me. "This one, however, needs an intervention."

Wait. What?

If we divide our crew up into saints and sinners, I'm the saint. Even my reasons for being on the lam are almost entirely benign, although I've kept those to myself. Lola's my girl, but we haven't known each other long enough to trade life-and-death secrets.

So I frown right back at her. *Deny deny deny.* "I'm an angel."

Lola reaches over and smacks my arm. Since she's already sitting super close, she comes close to honking my boob. "You kissed a boy."

This is *not* the moment to ask which boy because there are only two possibilities: my last kiss with the Douche or my first kiss with Mister Hotshot. So I suck it up and brazen it out.

"So?" That's a genius comeback right there. Short, pithy, and puts the onus back on Lola.

Of course she's up for the challenge. "Shall we review the rules of the Break Up Club?"

"Objection." Olivia's hand shoots up into the air. "Those rules were suggested steps, not stipulated regulations."

"Are you a lawyer? Judge? Jury? Long arm of the law?" Lola blows a raspberry—and Olivia sort of freezes.

"No?" Anybody hear the question in Olivia's answer?

Yeah, me too. Unfortunately, they both turn and stare at me. I'd rather pursue whatever Olivia's hiding.

"Sure?" I say rather weakly. The longer we review, the longer I have to figure out which guy Lola's up in arms about. I've spent loads of time recently getting creative with my life story, so I can deal with this.

Lola springs to her feet and starts pacing back and forth. I think she might have mistaken our rather grubby campsite for a Broadway stage because she pitches her voice to be heard by us and every wild animal lurking in the woods.

"Ladies, in order to be founding members of the

Break Up Club, you swore you'd lived through a particularly egregious break up. We agreed to get over those bad relationships together, to support each other, to make sure no member backslid."

I nod vigorously. "And I'm pretty sure I said *thank you*."

Thank you not being the same thing as *signed in blood*, but there's no stopping Lola. She marches over to the porch hanging off the front of her cabin and retrieves a large, pink sign. It's huge, but lighter than it looks—kind of like the men in my life. They've been well-hung but light on emotions and feelings. Olivia winks at me, while I wonder if there's a way to slink back to my cabin. I miss my stupid, lumpy mattress something fierce. Instead, I read obediently.

1. Accept the empty spots in your life: heart, head, bed, laundry basket, and that drawer in the bathroom you cleaned out just for him.

2. Cut it off. No texts, no tweets, no Facebook pokes, pings, or any other blip or beep on the social media radar. Distance is your new best friend and beer goggles have nothing on your

ability to overlook the 1001 reasons that relationship was doomed.

3. Feel it. Don't suppress! Let it all out!

4. No negative thoughts. Own your self-worth. Move out of the hermit shell and back into the real world. It's time to talk to people.

5. Be honest. Acknowledge why you broke up—and rip the Band-Aid off that sucker.

6. It's all about you. Self-improve, shop, and be nice to yourself.

7. Get back out there.

8. Onward! Upward! Don't look back. You've come this far, now be open to the possibilities.

"Are we on Step Seven?" Lola stabs the poster with her index finger and stares at me. Which is pointless. I am not the kind of person who remembers numbers. Or order. I can barely deal with the curveballs life has been lobbing at me lately, so I haven't been paying too much attention to steps one, two, and whatever. I've just been using the time to catch my breath and lay low.

"No clue," I lie.

Still…

I read the rule that Lola's now tapping with a dramatic finger. Step Seven. *Get back out there.* Uh, no. I've been doing my very best to stay *right in here*. Undercover. Sotto voce. *Not* drawing attention to myself. *Except for yesterday's slip up*, the little voice in my head chimes in. *The slip up where you accidentally on purpose gave tongue to Mister Hotshot.*

Yeah. Except for that.

"Class?" Lola points to Olivia, who's looking doubtful. I suspect she's the kind of person who will still be able to do calculus proofs when she's ninety.

"We're not on Step Seven," Olivia admits.

"But Sarah Jo has skipped ahead on us." Lola winks at me. She's not mad—just giving me a hard time. "She locked lips with a very sexy hotshot at fire camp yesterday, and then she kept the details to herself."

Pick, not the Douche. I inhale deeply and nearly choke on a nose-full of smoke. I've done plenty of things I regret in my life, but strangely enough, kissing

Pick is not one of those things. Not even close.

"I'm not getting back out there," I say firmly.

"But you did kiss the boy." She whips her phone out of her pocket and holds it up so I can see the screen.

FYI? When you kiss a guy in public with a half-dozen cooks egging you on? You should expect to end up on the Internet. So I'm not surprised, although I'm not trying too hard to see the evidence with my own eyes. I don't even like my own photos. I doubt I'll like watching myself kiss any better. Fortunately, my face is mostly obscured in the footage.

"Guilty as charged." I'm not convinced that confession is good for the soul. Frankly, I've been happier telling nothing to anyone.

"Was it good?" Lola passes her phone to Olivia. I think about trying to wrest it away from her, but I'm pretty sure she could kick my ass. Plus if Lola has the video, it's undoubtedly all over the Internet—or at least the local Facebook pages.

Olivia grins. "You can see that for yourself."

"Cannot." I give in and grab the phone.

Whoever shot this was expecting it. In the first frames, I'm standing with my butt to the videographer, who shoots over my shoulder as I strut up to Pick. He's so damned gorgeous. Even all mussed and sooty from the monster forest fire he'd just spent hours fighting, he looks ready for some hot loving. He's big and built, and he moves with that easy grace some large men have. He's comfortable in his own skin, and he doesn't care what anyone else thinks. If I didn't want to kiss him again so badly, I'd resent that.

Movie Star Me reaches up and drags Pick's head down to hers and proceeds to kiss him vigorously. I give myself points for effort. It's not the smoothest kiss I've ever seen, but it's clearly getting the job done. The phone disappears out of my hand.

"So?" Lola stares at me expectantly.

"It was a dare. I had to kiss the first guy I saw."

"Such a hardship," Olivia mocks.

"So you just tripped and your tongue accidentally ended up in his mouth?" Lola's not ready to let this kiss go.

"It was just a kiss." A really awesome, smoking hot, toe-curling first kiss—which is my favorite kind. It also sort of has me wondering what a second kiss with Pick would be like. I don't really want to admit this to Lola and Olivia because then they'll know that it wasn't *just* because of the dare.

"Just?" Olivia asks.

"It was nothing. Are we really meeting just to ask me about a ten-second kiss?"

Lola grins. "Are you really doing Step Seven without us?"

I take a moment to imagine the collective reaction of the Big Bear Rogues if the three of us (or the four of us if I include Hunter) descend upon them looking for a chance to *get back out there.* Honestly, they're nice guys. I'm sure they'd be happy to help strictly as a public service, but I don't really want my sex life to be a group project.

"He's not my Step Seven man," I say as firmly as I can. "He was an aberration, a mistake."

Lola nods thoughtfully. "Because it would be totally okay if you felt ready to get back on the horse."

From the way she waggles her eyebrows, I think we all know she means *horse* as in *hung like a horse*. But I've sworn off guys. Maybe not forever, but for at least a year or ten. Kissing Pick was fun—and he's a good sport—but I can't go back for seconds. He is *not* an all-I-can-eat buffet.

Even if part of me wishes he were.

"This is the intervention part, right?" Olivia looks at

Lola. When Lola nods, she continues. "Good. Then I'm going to tell you that you'd be crazy not to kiss your hotshot a second time. You only live once, and that man…

She makes a good point.

I need to stop.

Stop running.

Stop hiding behind my clothes, my hair, my fears.

And if it takes plastering myself all over a very sexy hotshot to do it? Well, there are definitely worse self-help programs in this world.

"I'll think about it," I say.

"Do it." Lola nudges my knee with hers. "No regrets, girl. If you want to Step Seven that hotshot, you do it. YOLO."

Lola screams this last word as she hoists her phone over her head. She looks like a warrior princess, a star, like a woman who's not afraid of anything. I'm so sick and tired of being scared all the time. That's not who I used to be, and I don't like who I've turned myself into. The old Sarah Jo didn't back down from a challenge. She went through life at full speed, living balls out. I'd kind of like her back.

SARAH JO

THE LOOK on Pick's face when I strolled away from him after our first kiss is priceless. Yes, that's *present* tense. Thanks to the miracle of modern cell phone technology, I'm able to replay that look of stunned surprise over and over again. I'm also the happy recipient of not one but two iPhone videos of his face and a third of his butt (the cook in question has a definite thing for faded denim and I'm not complaining). He looks amused. Deliciously confused. Ready to come after me and ask me all about my *specials.* It has to be the sensual warmth in his eyes, though, that has me melting. I kissed him on a dare, but I definitely don't need any more trouble. Or men.

So maybe I grabbed a screenshot from Rosalie's Pick video and made it my wallpaper. And just maybe one of the steamier stills is now hanging on the wall of the kitchen with *Dish of the Day* scrawled in the margins in hot pink Sharpie. I'm sure you remember that Pick is a good-looking man. Mr. Chocolate-Eyed, Broad-Shouldered, Big-Dick Lumberjack kisses even better than he looks, too, which is a definite plus in my book. It's too bad I can't start something with him, but I've learned my lesson. No more policemen, sheriffs, first responders, or firemen. That kind of guy is nothing but take-charge trouble.

Still, walking away from him was hard.

Especially since parts of me—the more southern parts—insist I should grab his hand and lock him in my cabin. He'd make one hell of an afternoon off.

On the other side of the camp, a car starts. I jump before I can stop myself and the silverware I'm holding bites it, scattering on the cafeteria floor. I look down at it. Yup. Dirty, dirtier, and dirtiest. I'll have to re-wash it all. Bending down, I scoop up the rejects and eye the departing vehicle as surreptitiously as I can. Just one of the hotshots leaving camp for an afternoon of R&R. A car pulling out—not *in*.

Still safe.

"Don't overreact," I tell the silverware. "He can't find me out here."

Okay—so it's *won't* and not *can't*. I'm pretty sure my ex could track me down in Antarctica if he put his mind to it. Thad Hill has the tracking skills of a bloodhound.

Unfortunately for my peace of mind, the sound of a second motor approaching the camp requires a recheck of the impromptu parking lot through the cafeteria's front windows. The battered pickup definitely seems like hotshot material. Hotshots don't make billionaire money, and they like their trucks tough and rugged, chosen for their ability to take on backcountry roads and haul loads. Like the men themselves. There's a certain raw beauty about that kind of dedication and power. Hotshots are men with staying power.

Unlike my ex.

Thad will come for me. Making like an ostrich won't change that truth. I should have known better.

Thad is law enforcement and I fingered him for a jewelry theft and cover-up arson . . . and then he deflected the blame back onto me. Nevertheless, the possibility of discovery seems far away right now. I'm three hundred miles away from Mr. Douche. Plus, the fire camp, for all its rough-and-tumble ways, is more peaceful than any town or city. Instead of skyscrapers, ponderosa pine reach for the summer sky, which is all hazy heat and summer gold instead of smog and light pollution. It's like I'm starring in my very own Disney movie because I can count at least a dozen different birds flying around and making mad, loud bird noises. Even the squirrels have glossy coats, for crying out loud. The place certainly smells a hell of a lot better as well.

Line cook isn't any harder than my last job as a home care worker. I had my own small business, taking care of a few elderly women. I met Thad when I picked up the phone and called for a wellness check for one of my ladies who hadn't answered the door or collected her mail. He arrived in uniform. Different from my usual dates, but he was polite. Considerate. My client was fine, but he kept on coming by. *Calling*, my ladies said.

Sniffing around, more like.

You know those truffle hogs that Frenchmen use to

dig up super expensive, ugly as fuck, but really damned tasty truffles? Thad is the ultimate truffle hog. He's all beady eyes and snuffling nose. You know, if he were a girl. I Googled it the other night when I couldn't sleep, and it turns out that truffle hogs are all females because truffles have some chemical in common with male pig saliva. You're confused? Welcome to my life.

Hog or not, Thad made his grand entrance into my life, and I greeted him like he was a tasty treat. He had the same reaction to me, which should have been my first clue. Small-town dating has never been my thing. I don't do sitting on the front porch or evening walks and sweet sunsets. I stuck out and not in a sexy or good way. After he met my Mrs. Joan when I was running late one night, his interest had done a 180. The elderly lady sat outside with him, wearing her "diamonds" and chatting Thad's ear off, while I finished up inside. Unfortunately, the only diamonds I'm familiar with are the tiny engagement rings my friends' fiancés buy at the local Sears. I had no idea that those big stones were *real*.

Yeah. Reality check.

Dragging my attention back to my new here-and-now, I dump the sullied silverware into the dirty bin and then add more clean forks to the pile I'm assembling for the dinner rush. Fifty should be enough. Eight hours into my shift, and quitting time is definitely on the horizon. I hate loose ends, though, so I'll finish the sorting, prep the tables for tonight's hungry hordes, and then clock out. After all, it isn't as if I have anywhere to go. My deluxe, five-star summer accommodations are that double bed in my just-big-enough-for-one cabin at Baby Bear Lodge. The cabins are named after the local wildlife, and of course I've been blessed with Beaver #1. The mattress sags something fierce, and the slippery art of keeping the sheets put still eludes me. So there you have it, folks. More forks, or an early night curled up in bed with a paperback.

Choices, choices.

Another car crawls up the rutted fire road, gravel crunching beneath the tires. Why am I working in Grand Central Station? This is Mountainsville, the capital of Nowheresville. There shouldn't be so much traffic. I don't have to look. I really don't have to.

Of course, I look.

How can I not? If my life were a horror movie, I'd totally go into that empty room or check out the nice, dark, spooky woods. And, oh, God, that *is* a patrol car. I can't read the words on the passenger side door, can't tell if this is the local sheriff or if Thad has found me. I recognize the cold clench of my stomach, followed by the wave of nausea. Today's lunch promptly transforms into one of those little rowboat things that the waves toss around ruthlessly. Still thinking I'm overreacting? Just wait until I hurl on your feet. Hoping stupidly for a coincidence, I crane my neck, trying to see.

Someone moves in behind me. Someone male and large, who's scuffing his feet deliberately because he's afraid he'll scare the shit out of me. The hotshots can be a real sweet bunch, but I've already overdosed on scared for today.

"Be right with you." I twist my neck wishing I'd paid more attention to that yoga thing Olivia had tried to teach me. Olivia's the second member of the Break Up Club, and she's a bit of a health and fitness nut. Where I'm a peanut butter milkshake, she's an organic kale smoothie. As you'd expect, I'm about as flexible as PVC piping, and I still can't get a good look at the car. Go. Stay. My body practically explodes trying to choose between fight or flight.

The car's driver is clearly male, but I can't make out anything else through the tinted glass. I'll have to wait for him to get out, and then I'll have only a few seconds to decide. It's not like I can announce that the good deputy is a thieving bastard. I already tried that and got precisely nowhere. Sure, I know that he broke into Mrs. Joan's house, stole enough jewelry to purchase a small island in the South Pacific, and then covered his thieving ass by setting the house on fire. Problem is, I caught him leaving—but I have no proof. It's my word against his. And no one believed me. My only consolation is that Mrs. Joan wasn't home—thank God for Bunco night at the senior center—so no one was hurt. Physically, at least. I imagine the older woman mourns the loss of a houseful of memories that no insurance check can replace.

I lean a little further.

Is the door opening? Is he just sitting there, trying to torture me? Maybe I should walk out with my hands up.

"Problem?" Oh, the surprise. The universe has decided to go all in on my helping of trouble today. Because that too-male, too-interested voice belongs to one Pick Revere. Like whiskey going down, his voice is all rough-smooth, golden edges. And just like whiskey, I'll have nothing but regrets in the morning.

I go with the safe answer. The so-not-true answer.

"Nope."

"You sure?" He sounds unconvinced—and concerned. As if he has a stake in my personal well-being, or at least some kind of interest. Plus, he's called me out on lying about my mood before.

Somehow, I'm even less surprised by his pursuing me than Thad. He might have removed his mouth from mine after our kiss, but he didn't pull back. Not really. I'd beat feet back behind my table ready to give the man all the pancakes he could eat, but he'd stood his ground. I'm pretty certain he'd been five seconds from clearing the table and repeating our kiss, and I hadn't known how to feel about that. Now, as he steps closer, I swear I can feel the heat of his big body despite the rapidly dwindling stretch of empty space between us.

And there's the desire I've been pretending doesn't exist, the insta-lust that just shouldn't happen to mostly-good girls who are trying really hard to start their lives over. I should pick a mantra. Some kind of reminder word that freaking encapsulates what I'm doing here.

Solitude.

Independence.

Absofreakinglutely.

Oooh, that last one is a good one.

Unfortunately, nothing seems to cure me of wanting to jump Pick and see if he'd be open to a game of hide-the-sausage. The extra dirty version, naturally. I remind myself that I've declared my independence from the male of the species. Every day is the Fourth of July on my calendar. I'm not dating, and I'm definitely not putting myself in another no-win situation with a take-charge alpha. Everyone here will take his word over mine any day of the week and twice on Sunday.

So there's the question I don't want to ask. Pick's the original bossy lumberjack. Take charge. I'd like to think I could hold my own, but I'm supposed to be flying under the radar in this camp, and there's no way I take him on quietly. Fighting with him would be fun. And taming the alpha male? Sign me up for that safari, please. It's just that I shouldn't. Not today, not tomorrow, not until I've somehow magically resolved this business with Thad. My hooha and my heart are officially closed for business.

None of which explains why my stupid head goes rebel and jerks around for a better look at Pick and is promptly rewarded for its foolishness. Pick is definitely worth looking at. His hair is damp from a recent shower, and a clean T-shirt clings to his powerful chest. No fancy words or logos for him. Just plain white cotton and blue jeans paired with practical steel-toes. Strong, tanned forearms cross over his chest as he watches me, his eyes narrowed. *Play it off.*

This would be more successful if my traitorous head doesn't swing back and forth between Pick's pretty face and the parking lot like a Wimbledon spectator.

"There's really no problem?" I have to give him credit. He sounds like he's at least trying to believe me. I promptly feel all warm and tingly inside because my stupid, stupid head is suggesting that we've just found ourselves a white knight and we should take full advantage. You know, ride off with him into the sunset of happiness, or at least ride him. Lady's choice, right?

"No," I repeat, a little more loudly than is strictly necessary. "I'm absolutely fine. My life is one big dream."

Liar, liar, pants on fire.

For *Pick*, those certain southern parts of me point out.

Nightmare alert, my head screams because it's hard to ignore the police when you're on the run, no matter how hot the local scenery is.

The patrol car makes that small pinging sound of a

vehicle that's been driven long, far, and fast. Funny how such a little sound still sounds like the trumpets announcing the start of the apocalypse. I can practically hear God going *told you so.* I'm such a bad country song. The po-po shows up, lights flashing, and I can't stop myself from flinching. Thank that laughing God that I don't play poker.

"Seems like it to me." Pick's right behind me now. "You're real tense."

Okay, Captain Obvious. Also, FYI? I'm revoking his credit for pretending to believe me when I said I was okay. Still, he wins some points back for his next move. A big hand walks down my spine, pressing out the knots. *Bliss*. Leaning into that hand would be too easy.

"Figment of your imagination." I pull away because I'm still wearing my big girl panties (despite the panty-melting qualities of my companion), tracking the car with my eyes. Will the door ever open? Why on earth is he just sitting there? Admittedly, even the non-penis-owning scenery up here is impressive, and lots of people like to ooh and ah over big, tall trees and the mountains, but still. He should get out. Move on. Do whatever it is that police officers get paid to do that does not involve arresting my butt.

Pick's hand comes back, landing on my shoulder. I do my best not to flinch. Just because I kissed him yesterday doesn't mean he has touching privileges now.

I'll use my words if I have to.

Of course, I also talked and talked that last time I visited the police station. I filled out forms and told them what I knew. Thad paid me a little visit that same night. He'd pulled up alongside me in his patrol car and snapped out an order to get in. At least he'd pointed toward the passenger side and not the back, in the Plexiglas cube where he locked up criminals. After I got in—and I should have started running *right* then—he threatened me. If I kept talking, he'd talk, too, and share his side of things. The whole time, his fingers clenched my arm, squeezing the bones of my forearm together. It hurt. It was like being in a bad movie, except we weren't at the happy ending right before the credits start rolling, when our heroine has overcome all the nasty shit life's dumped on her and hooked up with the hero. I was stuck in the part where she's lost all hope. I promptly panicked and ran as soon as he let me out.

I can't do that again.

Strike that. I *won't* do it.

New and improved me will stick up for herself or

get even or maybe consider mortgaging her soul to buy a remote castle with a really big moat. Then I can always pull up the drawbridge and wait trouble out.

"You know the county sheriff?" Pick's voice rumbles in my ear. Is it just me, or does he even sound sure and steady? Dependable. Protective. Like a total white knight, if you know, white knights were the size of mountains and rode Harleys in their spare time. Whereas I'm ready to run around in frenzied circles looking for an exit, he's not in any rush. The car door is definitely opening, the sound drifting through the cafeteria's screen door.

"Not me." God, I hope not.

"So there's no problem there. You didn't date and dump him, or bump into him in the supermarket and have to listen to his long-ass stories about fishing and now he's on your avoid-at-all-costs list."

Pick's drawl is slow and knowing. He knows he makes me nervous, and he knows I'm hiding something. In fact, he knows far too much. I open my mouth to say something, anything, because I know things, too. Like how to lie. It probably should bother me how easily the lies come, but I'm long past caring about ethics and moral values. You don't put caviar on your shopping list when you're down to your last dollar. Adrenaline spikes through my body, leaving me weak at the knees and painfully alive. Life is too short. Too uncertain. Blah blah freaking blah. Pick's big body brushes against mine because of course he hasn't stayed away, and I make the split-second decision to seize the opportunity. He's here, he's close, and if I don't have my way with my hotshot now, tomorrow might be too late.

Thad could find me tomorrow. And if not tomorrow, the calendar is full of alternative dates, all of which will end equally badly for me. The only safe moment is now. I have to stop freaking out at every little noise. This is no way to live.

And I really, really want to live.

The last few months I've been putting down the highway of life in an overloaded minivan towing a whole lot of baggage. I'm ready to upgrade to a Camaro. To something with sizzle and flash and fire. No more speed limits, no more detours, no more wishing I'd gone in a different direction.

I'm lonely, I want sex, and this big hunk of man mountain is checking all the boxes on my top ten sexiest man traits list. You think all those driving metaphors were bad? Well, I'm getting off the highway of fear.

Pulling over, making a pit stop, taking some *me* time.

This hotshot's mine.

"Sarah Jo?"

"Yeah?" Even the way he says my name revs me up.

"You dating the sheriff?" I can hear the amusement in his voice, along with something else. Something that's darker, hotter, and way more dangerous to my panties.

"No dating at all," I get out, before a big finger comes up and covers my lips.

"Better not to say anything, darling. Whatever you're coming up with, I'll wait for the truth."

PICK

SARAH JO bites me.

Not hard, but enough to make a dent in my finger that will be gone within the hour. I'm a tough son of a bitch, partly because it's a job requirement, but mostly because that's how life's made me. Teeth marks don't put me off. Fuck, part of me likes the fact that she's decided to sink her teeth into me. The rest of me knows I damned well deserve whatever she dishes up because I shouldn't be pushing her. Shouldn't be touching her yet since she hasn't issued an invitation.

Yet.

Hasn't issued one *yet*.

Apparently, I'm an eternal fucking optimist where this woman is concerned, too. Still, I move my finger. I'm not entirely certain she won't try to detach it from my body otherwise, and I have all sorts of dirty plans for that finger and Sarah Jo's body. I'd hate for her to miss out because I've been reduced to a nine-finger wonder.

Now that I've removed my finger from her person, her grip tightens on the pile of forks she's clutching like they're an arsenal of deadly weapons she just can't wait to launch. Possibly, she's entertaining fantasies of stabbing me. Although I'd rather she mentally undressed me and rode me like a cowgirl, I'll take what I can get. She's not ignoring me and that goes straight into the plus column in the Pick Revere Dating Ledger. Frankly, that ledger's been a little too empty lately. I haven't dated much in recent history—a fire call comes in and I go out, which makes me bad Friday-night fodder and a frequent flyer at the local titty bar where I can at least look if I can't touch—but even I know that paying attention is a good sign. Besides, I get the feeling that Sarah Jo doesn't do things the easy way. She won't be Friday night and a movie.

Or maybe that's just me, looking at her and seeing

something more. Maybe yesterday's kiss really was just a quick dare, a little fun that's over now and she's thinking *why the fuck isn't this guy moving along?* Maybe I'm the only one who sees her move as the opening gambit in something bigger. I liked the taste of her all right—and I definitely want more. I'm not settling for the one-scoop vanilla cone when I could have the entire fucking sundae *and* a cherry. I want her naked and underneath me. Or over, alongside, or reverse cowgirl. We can work our way through the entire Kama Sutra if she wants, even the crazy positions that would challenge an Olympic gymnast.

But instead of getting naked followed by getting down and dirty, she's tense and hyper-focused on the sheriff parked outside the building. I don't know why a police car has her jumping like fleas on a dog, but she's visibly a nervous wreck. Pretty sure she's trying to hide behind me, too. On the other hand? I can work with that. Shielding her from sight is simple enough, and letting her lean on me some is even easier. Hell, I can even admit that having strong, sassy Sarah Jo leaning on me gives me a primitive satisfaction and awakens a desire to take care of her. Whatever bad thing she feared isn't going to happen on my watch. It'll just be non-stop orgasms and good times.

You know what? I'm not sure where this urge to go all protect and defend on her came from. It's a little foreign when not applied to burning buildings.

Maybe it's because she definitely looks good enough to eat. Today she's wearing another sassy T-shirt—*Hugging a firefighter is hot*—and a matching skirt that clings to her ass and her thighs. An enormous flannel shirt is tied around her waist, her full-body camouflage shucked in deference to the already oppressive temperatures. Likewise, her bare legs sport flip-flops instead of boots because only a sadist or a hotshot would wear steel-toes in the triple-digit summer heat baking the camp. Missing her would be hard since her shirt is the most obnoxious shade of purple I've ever laid eyes on. I'm not certain she's wearing a bra beneath all that color, and I damned certain want to find out. So I rile her up just a little bit more.

"You still say there's nothing wrong?"

She moves then, putting me between herself and the car's line of sight. Obligingly, I step closer so my shoulders block the window. I'm such a fucking Boy Scout. Maybe she'll pin a merit badge on me later. With her mouth.

Sarah Jo doesn't strike me as the kind of woman who runs scared. She's more likely to kick trouble in the balls (and yes I'm watching mine), so I don't know what could have set her off so. It's just the county sheriff, doing his weekly drive-by and the other usual fire camp visitors. She's made it clear she isn't sharing, however, so I won't push.

Much.

"Not a thing," she says confidently, but then jumps at nothing, showering forks all over the floor. The clatter's loud enough that you'd think a one-man band just exploded or something. The move, however, puts her right in my arms. Her amazing tits brush my chest, and now I've got firsthand evidence that she opted out of wearing a bra today. There's a whiff of something citrus, too. Her shampoo, maybe, or lotion. Either way, she smells like she belongs on my menu. She's lunch and I should absolutely eat her up. And out. Fuck, yeah.

She slides her hands up my arms and over my shoulders, linking them around my neck. If she's omniscient *and* on board with my dirty plans for her, I'm the happiest man alive.

"You liked kissing me?" Not stopping for an answer, she abandons the forks and walks me toward the side door, her thighs pressing into mine with each step she takes. I have no idea where we're going but I'll let her lead in this little dance we've got going on. "The other day?"

I'd kiss her anywhere, anytime. I set my hands on her hips and let her steer me outside. I'd even be up for sex in public at this point because my dick's that damned hard.

No point in beating around the bush. "You know I did."

I have the feeling my mouth is opening and shutting in a troutlike fashion I'll regret later. Something about Sarah Jo knocks me off balance, starting with the unexpected offer coming out of her mouth. Apparently, she isn't waiting for *my* answer, however, because her fingers walk up my neck, find my ear like she owns it, and just like that I'm even harder. I *definitely* want to do that again.

And her. Performing wicked, naughty sex acts on Sarah Jo's willing body is high on my to-do list right now.

"My shift is over," she announces.

Does that mean what my dick is praying it does? Could be she's just making awkward conversation or is leading up to abandoning me and my hard-on, but it's hard to not be hopeful.

"Mine too," I growl. Meant that shit to come out as a whisper, something soft and teasing, but the blood's abandoned my brain and nothing about me is smooth and easy. Sarah Jo's fucking gorgeous, and she's got me so hot for her that I'm about to spontaneously combust. You think I should be romantic about this? Come up with some heartfelt compliments and do the woo? I'd like to, but my dick is in overdrive and this is so not what I thought would happen when I followed Sarah Jo into the cafeteria. I was planning on a beer and some dancing of the fully-clothed variety. I guess I shouldn't be surprised that a woman who would kiss me in front of an entire fire camp would also make it clear what the next step in our not-relationship should be. I like that she's not afraid to show me what she wants.

She dances me straight out the side door and into open air, executing a clever little twist that reverses our positions so I'm once again between her and the parking lot. Are you confused? So am I. Not sure if this is really about sex or not, but I can't help hoping. Which makes me an even bigger dick than I already am because if she's scared or worried about shit, I shouldn't be taking advantage of her.

I'm still wrestling with my inner good guy (FYI he's fucking losing), when she stops. Inner Good Guy abruptly comes over to the evil sexy hook up side when she goes up on tiptoe to peer over my shoulder, her pussy rubbing against my dick as she turns my body into her own personal ladder. "You know what's inside that cabin? Is it open?"

She points. I turn my head and look. Sooner or later, we're gonna have to have a conversation about who gives orders and who gets them.

Typically, my days start and end with the fire cache housed in the rundown wooden cabin at my back. Forty feet by forty, the one-room cabin is stuffed full of ordered supplies and twelve-packs of tools half-broken into, cardboard boxes and piles, piles, and more piles. When I'd opened the cache at the start of the summer, I discovered that someone had gone crazy with an ancient label-maker, sticking precisely lettered strips of black-and-white everywhere, although no amount of labels could ever corral the mess of Pulaskis and axes, sleeping bags and hard hats. Everything has been ordered in by the caseload and in multiples—and then left to explode everywhere.

"Supplies," I growl out, maneuvering her a little closer. Her hips are the perfect fit for mine—we slot together like two pieces in a sexy puzzle. But she's asked me a question, so I try to concentrate. Supply depot is definitely too fancy a term for what lies inside that cabin. More like *dumping ground* or *organizational nightmare*. Maybe, if there were fewer fires, I'd give a damn. And maybe pigs will fly.

She beams. "So it's empty."

If you count metal shelves crammed with crap empty, then, yeah. Totally empty.

She bounces against me, and turns up the wattage on her smile. I'm pig enough to ignore the forced cheer because holy fuck, the bounce move slides her pussy up and down the front of my jeans yet again, and I'm in unexpected danger of going off like a rocket.

She pats my chest. "Let's go in."

What the lady wants, the lady gets. I'm an absolute fucking gentleman like that. Possibly, I nod like a bobblehead because something about Sarah Jo short-circuits the thinking portions of my brain. Or maybe it's just that all available blood has stampeded south of my belt where there's a whole lot of happy and turned on going on.

She takes charge again, not waiting for my answer. That's fine. The only thing my mouth is good for right now is kissing and licking. Possibly also biting, moaning, and loving her good. My body doesn't mind the Sarah Jo takeover one bit. On the contrary, my dick jumps right to attention and my feet move doubletime. She sure is sexy. She slaps her hands against my shoulders, pushing me faster because she's impatient. I agree. Getting naked and closer is high priority. I move.

When my back hits an immoveable wall, I consider and then discard the idea of just picking her up and banging her against it. Wall sex is amazing, and she's so tiny that I could hold her up for hours. On the other hand, doing it for hours would put us on full display for the hungry hordes, and that has to violate about a hundred different HR rules. Might be a health code violation as well.

Since I like my job, I shove my hand down, feeling around the rough timbers for the doorknob. She takes charge of that, too, reaching around me, her fingers brushing against my ass as she pushes the door open.

And then she fucking shoves me inside.

Okay, so I go. Willingly. Apparently, I've answered my own question, and I'm up for a repeat of yesterday's kiss. I've tried being a responsible, mature adult and asking her what's wrong—because, clearly, something out there in the camp has spooked her bad—but she's made it clear that she doesn't want words. She went for my goodies instead, and I'm *so* on board with that plan. I'm even willing to let her sit in the driver's seat. Temporarily.

Yesterday's kiss was smoking hot, even with an appreciative audience. She apparently enjoyed kissing me because this unexpected lunch date in the storage cache proves I'm more than a dare and a drive-by kiss. Clearly, she's ready to give me a second shot, so screw Hunter and his claims that I was a throwaway and a convenient five minutes. I'm getting me at least an hour today—and a promise of more.

She two-steps me deeper into the cabin, her tongue tracing my lips.

"Making me work for it, Pick?" She whispers the teasing question against my mouth, and I smile. She has no idea.

"You're always welcome, honey."

My ass bumps up against a desk shoved along the wall, and my dick suggests we take full advantage of the horizontal surface. Good plan. I sweep one hand beneath me, ignoring the clatter of office supplies biting it. I'll sign on for pickup detail. Later. Right now, I park my ass down and pull her between my legs.

It's my turn to kiss her.

She doesn't make it easy. I don't mind the unexpected hookup, but the cabin isn't aces in the romance department. Chockablock full of card tables and shelves loaded down with extra handles and oil, wedges and spray paint, the few visible inches of the walls are papered with less-than-sexy park posters. A graffiti-covered Smokey the Bear stares at us, surrounded by fire road signs and maps bristling with pushpins. Those are souvenirs and victories right there, half covered with flight maps and helicopter schedules. I've been in here hundreds of times, and it's never looked so good as it does now that she's here with me.

"Sarah Jo," I say roughly, threading my fingers through her hair. Her name comes out half plea, half demand. We're still fighting to see who gets to be in control of what's happening here, and for the first time in my life, losing doesn't seem so bad.

"Don't talk." She leans in closer, her tits squashed up against my chest. She has to feel the massive boner I've got for her, but she doesn't seem to mind. In fact, she gives a little wriggle, like she's checking my stuff out and so far, so amazing. Her words trail off in a little moan-sigh.

"You don't want to slow things down?" Asking the question sucks, but informed consent is non-negotiable. Once I get the verbal go-ahead, I've got plans to strip off her clothes, lay her down on the floor, and go at her despite our potential audience outside the cabin. I'd be happy to draw you a flowchart, but showing you will be so much better.

"Not a chance," she growls. "I've decided that life is too uncertain not to take what I want, and you're first on my list."

I admire her priorities. Better yet, she slaps her hands down on the wall behind the desk, pinning my head between her palms. This is new. I take a second to appreciate my position. Usually I'm on top and in charge, but I'm willing to let her hold the reins for a moment. It helps that she's looking at me like I'm the center of her universe, and she's in a mood to explore.

Sure enough, she eliminates all remaining distance between us, pulling us closer together until there's not an inch of space left. I can't help groaning, which makes her smile. Naughty girls get what they have coming to them, and I have plans for Ms. I-Started-This Sarah Jo. Needing to touch her, to feel her hair, her skin, down her back, and over the soft crease of her hip, I reach for her. Behaving myself is no longer an option.

"See?" Her eyes light up with humor even as her fingers find my shoulders and squeeze. I squeeze back, but since my hands are on her spectacular ass, it's her turn to groan. "Talking's over-rated."

The lady is always right. Have I mentioned how much I believe that? She follows up the groan with a whimpering sound as I touch her more. Running my palms over her perfect curves. Pulling her closer, sliding my fingers beneath the hem of her shirt because I need bare skin, now.

She's hungry for me, too. The gentle shoulder squeeze turns dirty, her hands sliding slowly lower, yanking me close. She's not tall. She has to tip her head back to make eye contact, but we've got enough light, even with the door shut, that I can see her clearly. She gives my face another once over, and then smiles. Her hands move. Skim over my shoulders. Down my arms until her fingers tangle with mine.

She makes me feel… Christ, I've never deliberately set a fire outside working hours, but I suddenly know how an arsonist must feel. It feels so goddamned good to go up in flames, to make her burn.

"I'm right here." My voice sounds rough. "Right where you put me, babe."

She grins. "I'll make sure you don't mind."

Mission. Accomplished. She sends her hands roaming over my body like she wants it all right now. Over my shoulders and down my chest, yanking up my T-shirt and smoothing her fingers over my abdomen. Slowly because Sarah Jo's a masterful tease. Yeah, it's that good. She pulls me into her embrace and then our lips meet and we're devouring each other, hungry and urgent.

Turns out Sarah Jo doesn't take orders. Or directions, suggestions, or hints. Her tongue strokes mine boldly, taking my mouth exactly as she pleases while her hands go on a wicked, wicked walkabout. I have no complaints, but no way I get mine before she does. It's that gentlemanly code of conduct I can't quite seem to shake. Fortunately, although I'm not more determined, I *am* both bigger and stronger. I flip her around, laying her back on the table in one smooth move, pinning her hands.

"Kisses first," I whisper roughly.

"Pick." She gasps my name, trying to reach for me. I'd like to give in, give her what we both want, but I have to make this the most amazing fucking first time ever because I already know I want a second and a third chance. Is a million too ambitious? Because I can't imagine not wanting more Sarah Jo over and over.

So I hold her hands over her head. "Ladies first."

Before she can protest, I let go and drop to my knees in front of her. If she wants kisses, I'll give her kisses.

SARAH JO

PICK KISSES his way down my body, a hotshot on a mission. God, I could watch him for hours—and not just because he's sporting a most impressive erection. His new position—going down on me, be still my quivering hooha—lets me appreciate the downright enormous ridge beneath his jeans as he drops lower. It's my good fortune that the man's built to scale. The hard length presses first against my belly, my thigh, then is gone all together. Well crap. Now that he's let go, I try to steer him with my hands, wanting his face back within kissing distance, but he gently brushes me away.

"Let me make this good," he says. I'm dying, and

he's laughing.

"It's your job to put out fires," I point out, sounding downright freaking virtuous. "Chop chop."

He outright laughs this time. God, I love that raspy sound, half amusement, half growl. "You got to trust me."

"Now," I demand, because this is my *carpe diem* moment and he's withholding orgasms, but there's no hurrying Pick up. He's as methodical and thorough about this as he is about fighting fire.

While he explores the soft curve of my belly—God, I should have bothered more with sit-ups—his hands discover my breasts and rub over the cotton T-shirt, thumbing my nipples in a deliciously rough caress. You think he could take a hint from the words embroidered over my boobs, but maybe reading isn't on his mind right now. Torturing me is. The best, most delicious, sinfully erotic torture mankind ever devised. He teases and pinches, rubs and pulls, until my nipples seem to have a one-way connection to my clit, and everything in me is pulling tighter and tighter in the best possible way. And he's in absolutely no hurry at all, damn him. He devours me, like I'm the tastiest dish on today's menu. As if he's starving—for me. He strips off my shirt, licking, kissing, and nipping his way from one boob to the other. He likes what he sees, and he loves what he's doing, and me? I just melt in his big, capable hands.

Then finally, finally he's moving all the way down, his head dipping lower as his broad shoulders pushed my thighs apart. For a moment, I stiffen, not quite certain how far I really want to take this, but he pushes gently and I give, leaning up on my elbows, watching him. He's freaking amazing, so screw resistance, self-control, or discipline. I'm going to eat him up like he's the biggest, baddest, most sinful piece of cake ever.

I think he's in full agreement with me, too. He eases the skirt up over my knees and thighs until the fabric pools on my stomach.

"Watch," he orders.

He didn't just say that, did he? I just want to come, not reenact *Fifty Shades of Grey*. I don't like orders or not feeling in control. But then he blows lightly, sending shivers through me. Okay, so now isn't the time to bring up my issues.

He doesn't wait for me to agree or disagree, just runs a thumb over my thong. The feel of that light touch drives me crazy. Makes me groan. I didn't plan this, I swear, not until I spotted the car driving up, and even then I was running on instinct and relief. I just wanted to grab everything I could before time ran out and my life was game over. Thank God my panties are good ones, a sea foam kind of color, the edges trimmed with lace and a perky white bow. He's staring at them like I've got the Sistine Chapel wrapped around my hooha. His eyes darken and his breath catches.

"Pretty," he groans. "You know how badly I want to get underneath those panties, Sarah Jo?"

"Tell me." That's my voice that sounds so breathless and out of control. I'd do anything if he'd just keep touching me.

He does. I don't know if he's a mind reader, or just as desperate as I am. He drags his thumb down the very center of my panties and I moan.

"The whole fucking mountain could go up in flames right now, and I'd still be right here." He slides his hands under my butt, lifting me toward his mouth.

I squirm because we've got a few logistical issues here. He hasn't taken the panties *off*. His fingers cup and curl, teasing and stroking. And yet my panties stay firmly put. I'm giftwrapped for him, and all he's doing is shaking the package because he knows what's inside—and is going to make me *wait*. Damn him.

"What are you doing?" I ask the stupid question because, hello, I need an answer now.

"Wait and see." He flashes me a grin, the bastard. "If you still have questions in a minute, I'm not doing this right."

His hands didn't stop lifting, either. Guess that's my first clue. I could try wriggling out of them myself but this isn't the most secure position in the world. He touches me, and I moan again. He leans closer, his shoulders pressing my thighs apart as his mouth skims over my panty-clad center. I want him to lick me. To tongue me hard, to shove his face down, and make me forget about everything bad in the world. He could do it, too.

I've never felt like this. No man has ever made me want to have sex so badly. I've never been this desperate for an orgasm. And then his mouth... God... his mouth is right *there.* Pressed against the center of my panties. He's every bit as good—or as bad—as he's been promising because I go up in flames. I pull him closer, pleading for more. Or everything. Anything. My reward is a small, secret kiss I feel deep in my core. He has his palms wrapped around my butt cheeks, his fingertips tickling the crease between them and when he inhales, he has to smell me. Instead of being embarrassed, though, I'm aroused.

"Open up more," he growls.

Bossy, isn't he? I hesitate just a moment, thighs tensing against his shoulders before I give up and give in. I open my legs wide. He immediately rewards me for that obedience, moving higher, his fingers curling into the hot, salty spot where my thighs meet.

"Farther," he coaxes, nudging me. Anything. I'll do anything to keep him right there. Never mind that I can feel the cool surface of the metal desk beneath my butt and there's a ridge of fabric jammed at the base of my spine. It would have been smarter to jump him at a Four Seasons, but we're here now, and I'll kill him if he doesn't finish what I started.

"Did you lock the door?" Yes. I have to ask, even if I kind of hope he ignores my question. Or just tells me that yes, of course he did, and he's got a tank or something equally impenetrable (har) blocking the entrance to our impromptu love nest. Lies. Truth. All I want is plausible deniability and the green light to go ahead. This is the best worst idea ever, and I totally blame his hot physique and that unexpected flash of caring. How was I supposed to resist?

Unfortunately, he lifts his head. An inch. Crap. "Do you care?"

That's not a *yes*. In fact, I could probably infer it's a *fuck no because you didn't give me a chance, babe*. The problem is that I can feel each one of those three words on my skin. His breath brushes over me in a dirty, wicked tease. Do I care? Yes, I decide reluctantly. I do. Despite the fire camp baking outside in the summer heat, the air in the cabin feels shockingly cool on my bare skin. Which is bare because my skirt is hiked up to my waist and I'm using Pick's shoulders as my own personal footrest. I lift my hands. Set them down. Consider crossing them over my boobs. Why is casual hook up sex so goddamned awkward?

He takes pity on me. "No one's coming through that door. You can relax."

Right. Because stopping and having a conversation in the middle of hot, impulse sex-on-a-desk is so relaxing making. He must correctly interpret the look on my face, because he lowers his head and hooks my waistband, his thumbs drawing my panties down. The fabric teases me where I'm slick and swollen, pulling over my swollen flesh. He doesn't take them off, though, just leaves them tucked below my mound like now that he can reach what he wants, nothing else matters.

Thank God. We're done passing the appetizers around, and now we're going for the main course. I expect him to hop up, grab a condom, and get down to it, but instead he swipes his tongue over me. Oh. FREAKING. Yes. I suddenly understand why the hotshot team is sort of legendary all over town. If his teammates are anywhere near as talented, it's amazing anyone ever lets them out of bed.

Sensation bursts through me, pleasure following each sure lick. No more thinking. No more worrying. I fall back—forgetting all about my metal bed—grab his head with my hands, and turn him into my own personal steering wheel. Left, a little more to the right, and then right. Fucking. *There.* I yank him closer and let him hear my appreciation of his insane oral skills.

Once again, Pick proves he isn't a man in a rush. Again and again, he kisses me while I bump and grind, riding his amazingly talented face to the best of my abilities. He's admirably thorough too. He swirls his tongue around the top of my girl bits, drawing torturous circles around my clit before making the trip back down like he has all the time in the world and it's no rush, nowhere to be but here as the sweet, slow ache builds in me.

At some point, he's set me down on the desk because now he's got two hands at his disposal and God, can he use them. He slides his thumbs up, loving the hell out of my pussy. When he presses inside me with one callused finger, I see stars. And then I do some more groaning and demanding because why settle for looking at the Big Dipper when you could have the entire galaxy? I try to explain that to him, but my mouth seems incapable of anything more than babble and throaty moans. I run my hands all over him, touching each inch that I can, feeling up his arms, his shoulders, the top of his head. More Pick, please.

And he gives it to me. "Let go. Lean on me a little. No worries, honey."

It's rather obvious that I have worries, an entire tanker truck load of them, but I try to let it all go. His finger pushing back inside me again helps a whole lot with my attempt, because God bless the man, he finds my G-spot like he's got his own personal map of my body with a big X marking all my favorite, dirty spots. I come so fast that I surprise myself, grinding hard against his mouth and moaning his name.

Yeah. I just did that. I grabbed a guy, dragged him into some kind of storage shed, and proceeded to use him as my own personal dildo. It sounds kind of bad when I think about it like that. Whatever else he is, Pick's a decent guy, and he deserves more than being my police evasion tool. Like a matching his-and-her orgasm. He *totally* deserves that.

It takes me a moment to come down from cloud nine or wherever it is that Pick's magic tongue has catapulted me to. I'm sort of hanging onto his head, alternating between patting it and pulling on it. Hopefully, I haven't snatched him bald, but he's certainly to blame. He made me see stars, and he made me lose control. Any resulting bald patch is just the price of entry.

And… he's watching me. I mean, that's better than having him stare at my post-orgasm cooter, but it's a little unnerving. I've spent most of my time recently doing my best to hide in plain sight, and rule number one of hiding is don't attract attention. I should say thank you. Or praise his mad oral skills. Something. Anything. Instead I blurt out one word.

"What?"

Awesome. I could have gone with that one. Or

fantastic. Mind-blowing. Even without the thesaurus app on my phone, I have to be able to come up with a dozen more flattering words to hit him with. He doesn't look offended, though. He just keeps on staring, although his hands drift lower, running over my inner thighs and making little shivers run up and down my back. It's both relaxing and arousing at the same time, which explains why my eyes start drifting shut. After the monumental orgasm I've just had, a nap sounds perfect. I know I should move, should return the favor, but he's reduced me to this boneless pile of limp.

"You don't like being told what to do." He slips the casual observation in, like he's telling me something I don't know.

I force my eyes open and attempt to multi-task, wriggling back enough to sit up and slam my shameless thighs shut. My inner hussy has been exposed enough for today, thank you very much.

"Why would I?" I'm sure he's not a fan of order-taking, if we're swapping secrets here, so why should I like it any more than he does?

He laughs, rocking back on his heels. Yes, I shoot a look at his crotch, trying to check out the goods. As far as I can tell, he's abnormally blessed in the downtown department. Super shlong, packing, hung. "Sometimes, taking orders can be fun."

I'm about to ask him for an example because I still have my doubts that he's ever taken orders and enjoyed it, but the dinner bell rings outside and someone hollers my name. Real life is about to come a-knock-knocking on the door.

"I need to go." Wham, bam, and thank you sir, but we're done here. In reality, after hiding in plain sight for so long, I'm feeling a touch *too* exposed now that he's been eye-to-hooha with me. A little strategic retreat is in order

"Gotcha." He pushes to his feet, the masculine grace and raw power of that big body kicking my senses into overdrive again. Or maybe I'm just disappointed that I'm going to have to make do with appetizers and not the main course after all because so much for having sexcapades. "Looks like I have a date with dinner after all."

"We're not dating." It's hard to sound dignified and in control when he gives me a hand off the desk and stands me up. Plus, I'm still super wet from his attentions, and there's an embarrassing noise I can't and won't place. At least I don't have sperm running down my legs, right? I try to lunge for the door, but my panties are still down around my thighs, and the sudden movement throws me off balance. Rather than face plant, I catch myself on his shoulders before I even realize what I'm doing. I'm grace incarnate and so not-sexy. Oh well, right? He adjusts my panties matter-of-factly, but then he squeezes my ass gently and points me toward the door. I think…

I have no freaking idea what to think.

"Whatever you say, honey."

PICK

THE FIRE CAMP at Big Bear Lake isn't precisely easy to find, and the two-lane highway that dumps visitors out at the ranger station near the park's entrance is a poor excuse for a road. Most folks end up cranky as fuck, and from the dust coating the sheriff's cruiser that pulls into the parking lot the day after I make Sarah Jo see stars in the storage shed, this newest of visitors hit every pothole and then some. Hope the taxpayers sprang for high-end suspension on that car because otherwise its driver has to be both shaken and stirred. You need a truck out here, one with four-wheel drive. We're not Kia country, and our rides have one job: to get us from camp to the fire and then to haul our asses out double-time when it's either quitting time at the zoo or the fire overruns us.

Not sure what's up with the cruiser, though. I spot a full rack of shotguns as if the good officer had prepared for bear or Armageddon. There's no snap-crackle-buzz of the radio, either. I'm betting this guy's running dark, which may have something to do with the name painted on the side of the car. He's across his county line, and he doesn't have jurisdiction this far southwest. I'm betting, however, that he's got something to do with Sarah Jo being jumpy as fuck yesterday—jumpy enough that she'd dragged me into the storage cache and had her wicked way with me. I probably shouldn't have done that, that whole letting her seduce me and ride my face thing. But it's hard to regret when I imagine I can still taste her every time I lick my lips.

So I watch as the officer finally opens the door and stands up, adjusting his uniform. Despite however long he's been sitting around with his thumb up his ass, his pants still hold a perfect crease and his utility belt is a thing of beauty. In addition to his semiautomatic, he sports what looks like a department-issue baton, a pair of cuffs, and a Taser. He still looks like a douche, though. Like he thinks he's in charge of All The Shit and he's just looking for an excuse to haul your ass down to the station in the back of his car.

I know what he sees when he looks around. The Bears' Lair, aka fire camp, is a sleepy dot in the middle of nowhere. This is our downtime space, the spot where nothing happens, and we fucking love it that way because out in the field hell is either breaking loose or you're mopping up after the last break out. Camp is a handful of weathered wooden buildings and a patch of gravel mostly filled with beat-up trucks and a few Japanese imports. A dented POS peels out of our impromptu lot, a foreign car from overseas with good mileage and a decent resale value. There's a little *fuck you* spit of gravel as the driver leaves the parking lot too fast.

I'm betting that's Sarah Jo leaving. I could will her to stay all I wanted, but she'd been scared yesterday and itching to go.

The Douche pauses next to his car like he's expecting a marching band welcome or celestial trumpets announcing his arrival. He's gonna be waiting a long time. I count it off, one one thousand, two one thousand... Get to fucking thirty before he gives up on anyone pulling a meet-and-greet and scans the buildings. He hasn't spotted me yet. Instead, the cabin door next to the cafeteria seems to catch his eye. Someone has added a neat sign saying MAIN OFFICE. Honestly, that someone is messing with The Douche because none of us are office types, and that office is empty. Everyone's either eating or out in the field.

I saunter over to intercept the man before he can spoil anyone's lunch. I'm such a saint—my boys can thank me later for taking one for the team. The good deputy spots me when I start moving, and promptly comes to a halt, waiting. He clearly thinks he's pulling a genius power play by making me approach him, and I'm itching to disabuse him of that idea. Preferably with my fists, although my feet wouldn't mind getting in on the action and kicking the shit out of him, either.

He looks complacent as fuck. He's tall, but not as tall as me. Bet he hates having to tilt his head back to make eye contact with me, so I get right up in his space. He's the kind of pretty boy that looks like he belongs on a billboard advertising cologne or tighty-whities. His dark hair is slicked back from his face, and he's got a real nice pair of cheekbones and a perfect nose. You know Humperdink in *The Princess Bride*? This guy could be his doppelganger, except without the velvet and lace.

"What's up?" I come to a stop when moving another inch would put my steel-toes on top of his shiny, hi-gloss loafers. Leaving my footprint there would practically be charitable of me because then his ass will have a nice keepsake of his time with us.

"Deputy Thad Hill," the Douche announces in self-satisfied tones. This is apparently my cue to fall down and worship, or at least show him the kind of respect I'd give my president or commanding officer. He must have the world's smallest dick, given the amount of compensating he's doing. I, on the other hand, know I'm hung. God's been over-generous in the dick department, and so I don't need to get into a pissing contest here.

The Douche then proceeds to trot out a badge case, just in case I have any doubts that my presence has been blessed with greatness. He flips it open smoothly, flashing a square of laminated, official looking plastic at me. His creds certainly look genuine, although there's always the possibility that Deputy Douche (to give him his official job title) is a fake with the real article.

Deputy Douche flicks the case shut and slides it into his back pocket.

We look at each other for a moment. Eh. Fuck it. I'd like to eat lunch, and I'd also like to go after Sarah Jo. Sleep, a shower, and a cold beer are high up on my to do list as well, so Deputy Douche needs to get on with it.

"You got business here?" Looming over him is ridiculously easy. Bet Deputy Douche is wishing he'd met a smaller hotshot or put lifts in those fancy shoes of his. Deputy Douche isn't a small man, either, but I have the advantage, the biggest one being that I don't have to pretend to be nice. Or *professional*. Even if Hunter Black is off-site at the moment and that makes me the man in charge. Which is very convenient when Deputy Douche shoves a picture in my face.

"No autographs," I tell him, enjoying the way he chokes on his righteous indignation. I'm not sure why I'm baiting him. Normally, I have nothing but respect for law enforcement—they do an important job, and like my hotshot team, their number one goal is keeping people safe. I admire that. This guy, however, rubs me the wrong way.

The photo is also a problem. I snatch it out of his hand and head into the office just in case that wasn't

Sarah Jo getting the hell out of Dodge a few minutes ago. I also think I'm not going to want an audience for this conversation because that's definitely Sarah Jo in the picture. Her hair's a little less colorful, but she's beaming at the camera with her trademark smile, flashing her fingers in a vee for victory gesture. She looks happy and way the fuck less haunted.

Her expression's almost as good as the one she sported yesterday after my tongue and I got done expressing our heart-felt appreciation for her pussy. Fuck, but she tasted good. Probably a good thing we didn't get around to actual penetration because she's obviously in an emotionally vulnerable place. You can't believe I just said that? That makes two of us. But banging the hell out of her on a desk when she was scared shitless about something didn't sit right then, and it doesn't feel any more right today. Sure, I've got regrets. My dick's been sending urgent messages to my brain since we parted and my balls are permanently Smurf-colored.

But even if *scared* and *sexy* can co-exist, I feel like I should take care of the *scared* thing first for her. Must be because I've still got a gentlemanly side and if she's not worried, she'll be able to focus all her considerable attention on the amazing orgasms I'm giving her. Who wouldn't want his best work appreciated? Just thinking about her spread out on the desk gets me hard all over again. Hope Deputy Douche doesn't think the hard-on's for him and end up with his precious feelings crushed.

"I'm investigating an arson." Deputy Douche obviously expects his pronouncement to be greeted with a chorus of Hallelujahs because my continued silence makes the other man blink. Which is why I continue keeping my mouth shut and wait. Sooner or later, Hill will tell me what I need to know. Then I can assess my options, fix whatever shit Sarah Jo's landed in, and go after her for round two in O-ville.

Hill fidgets. *Gotcha.* "You run into much arson up here?"

He's standing in the middle of a fire camp—we're a goddamned fire buffet up here. There are plenty of ways a wildland fire gets started, and arson ranks right up there at the top of the list. Idiots with matches, campers who think a no-burn rule doesn't apply to them, lost hikers who decide building a big-ass signal fire will get them out of the woods faster, firefighters who want the overtime or the experience… it's a crowded list.

"We've got plenty of fire up here," I allow.

Hill shakes his head. "Not a Big Bear kind of blaze. My fire is three hundred miles northeast of here."

The downright possessive tone in Hill's voice sets off all kinds of alarms. An officer of the law shouldn't be nosing around here without some kind of professional reason, but this doesn't sound like a routine investigation at all.

"Have you seen this woman?" Hill trots the line out like he's starring front and center in a bad television show. Just in case I'm terminally stupid, he taps the photo I've set down on top of the desk.

I'd sort of guessed based on her reaction to the sheriff's car yesterday that she was on the run. Turns out I'd also harbored a stupid hope that she'd let me in on the reasons why before law enforcement showed up for her. It's easier to hide the bodies before they're on public display, you feel me?

"You looking for her?" I counter, already running options in my head. Outing Sarah Jo to this man isn't happening. There's something off here, and I learned years ago to listen to that little voice in my head. My subconscious processes way before the facts reach the rest of my head—there's probably a big, fancy study backing me up, but this is experience talking, too. So, if my gut insists there's something wrong, my head's gonna listen.

"Sure am." Hill's thumb strokes over the glossy and I get the bad feeling that he's imagining that he's touching my girl. "Sarah Jo here is wanted for arson. She burned down the house of a little old lady she took care of."

"The lady get hurt?" Christ, I hope not. Whatever happened, Sarah Jo doesn't need to carry that burden, too.

Hill shakes his head. "Just a whole lot of property damage. You know where Sarah Jo is?"

"Can't help," I say blandly. More like, won't, but no point in tipping my hand to Hill just yet.

"No?" Hill sounds skeptical. Guess he's not as stupid as he sounds. "Because I'm fairly certain she's up here."

"Let's call in the boys, then," I suggest. "See if they've got anything to say."

Deputy Douche thinks this is a fantastic idea, even if I did come up with it myself, so that's what we do.

The reaction of the other hotshots when they pile into the cabin says plenty, too. My boys don't like the newcomer. Thad Hill is a slick, friendly guy, but he's also a little too friendly. One by one, each hotshot admires Sarah Jo's picture, a few of them a little too much (Colt actually asks for her number as if Deputy Douche is running a dating service), but all of them insist that they've never, ever seen her. They fucking lie like champs and I love them. Deputy Douche gets visibly frustrated as he gets one no after another, which is entertaining for the first ten minutes but ten gets old. Twenty Questions is so not my favorite game—that would be Truth or Dare, dirty style. Muttering a quick excuse, I leave Hill to wrap up his interrogation and head out for the cooks.

The good thing about those gals is that they're easy to find. Unlike my team, which can be almost anywhere along a fifty-mile fireline, cooks tend to be found near stoves, sinks, and large collections of knife blades. Blowing through the door of the cafeteria, I step into the path of the first cook I spot. She wisely comes to a halt rather than slamming into me because I seriously outweigh her.

I've got just one question. "What does Sarah Jo drive?"

The cook eyes me suspiciously for a long moment. Yeah. She's aware of Deputy Douche's surprise visit, and now she's calculating whose side I'm on. This isn't a playground, and we aren't playing boys against girls. I give her a nice, sexy, *calm* smile. A smile that promises we both want what's best for Sarah Jo. Safe and happy, right? And if I plan to ensure happiness with my mouth, fingers, and dick, that's nobody's business but mine and Sarah Jo's. Before any orgasms can happen, however, I have to catch up with her first.

"Honda Civic," she says finally, when I sling an arm around her shoulder and wink at her, tacitly promising that Deputy Douche isn't getting within a hundred yards of our girl.

My cook prefers words to coded gestures, however, because she proceeds to spell our agreement out. "You going after her—or selling her out to that *man* over there?"

She nods toward the office where Deputy Douche is exiting. He looks distinctly unhappy. Colt marches along on one side of him, and Kade brings up the right. Kade's the new boy on the team, and he was something hush-hush in the US military before he joined us, so he must know at least a dozen ways to kill a man and that's fine with me. Leave nothing to chance. They'll see him off and make sure he leaves. Also, FYI? Thad Hill had better not accept any offer of coffee these ladies make him, because the cook leaning into my side is definitely out for blood. She's a fucking amazing woman.

As is the one I've temporarily misplaced. As soon as I catch up with her, I plan to point out that I've got her back, even if she's not ready to open up anything more than her legs. So sue me. I'm not a poet. Hallmark wouldn't hire me if I were the last person left on Earth (although I guess they wouldn't need greeting cards then, would they?). What I'm trying to say is that I'll take sex for now, but I'd like to get inside her head and maybe her heart. Just a little and whenever she's ready. I'm a patient man and I know how to wait.

I let the cook go, dropping a kiss on her cheek. These ladies rock. "I'll always go after her."

Truth.

SARAH JO

THE HARLEY comes up fast behind me. The powerful cycle devours the road, easily chewing through the small distance I've managed to put between myself and the camp. Low-slung with a custom black paint job, the bike pales in comparison, however, to the helmeted man riding it. Pick hugs the powerful machine with his legs, all black leather and raw power. He looks hot.

Good enough to eat.

And almost-sex with Pick rocked my world in more ways than one yesterday. I'd pulled him into the storage shed because I'd known I was running out of time, so I'd planned on taking what I could. If you only get one pass through the world's best buffet, you load up your plate and you start with dessert first. Screw vegetables and eating what you should—you go for the good stuff and you shovel it in. Life's too short not to get my hands all over my hunky hotshot. What I hadn't expected, however, was that Pick would make me feel like something besides a mind-blowing orgasm. Why does he have to be so hot? And so freaking sweet underneath that tough guy exterior? He makes me dream about curling up next to him, into him. Letting him take care of me as I pour out my worries and concerns. I can't explain why I feel this way, but I know it's a mistake.

In fact, it's a super familiar mistake, and one I swore I'd never make again. There are plenty of enjoyable uses for the penis-owning members of society, but expecting them to stick around and partner up isn't happening. So that makes my fascination with Pick pure trouble.

Pure temptation.

I can ignore him, right? That's a possibility. I've left camp so it's not like I'm on pancake duty. He has no business following me, plus I could always argue that I didn't recognize him with the helmet on. Driving on and on is a tempting thought. I cranked the radio up as soon as I cleared the parking lot and Thad's line of sight, going pedal to the metal somewhere else. Anywhere else. Unfortunately, the near-empty gas gauge reminds me that I'll need to refill before I do too much more driving. I'm certainly not making it to Mexico before I'm coasting on empty.

Driving like a mad woman isn't the wisest of moves, but I'm not going to lie to myself. Thad scares me. He wields his badge like a weapon, and I'm in his sights. He's already insinuated that I can make up my bad behavior in the backseat of his patrol car. After I'd peeled away from the camp, it had taken the next fifteen miles of windy, twisty highway to get my panic under control.

I half expect Pick to pass and cut me off, but instead he drops in behind my Honda. Not crowding my bumper any, but right up on my butt where I can't possibly miss him. He flashes his lights and jerks a thumb to his left. Once. Twice. Part of me agrees that talking might be smart. That's a very small part, however. The rest of me remains convinced that the faster I run, the better. Mexico looks better and better the more I think about it.

They have beaches, margaritas, and an unlimited supply of colorful fish I can hang out with. Of course, it would mean life on the run, and I'm fairly certain I'd be violating like a million Mexican immigration laws. And I'm broke. Driving an ancient Honda Civic that has two gallons of gas left. I flip the turn signal on and ease my foot off the gas.

Running forever isn't feasible. I know it, you know it, and now Pick knows it.

Twenty yards of guardrail and mountain give way to a small turnout. Bingo. I pull off carefully because dying now isn't part of my plans, either. A small placard declares this to be a Scenic Spot, and sure enough, there's one hell of a view. Other than the generous helping of outdoors beauty, however, there's not much. Just a few yards of rutted gravel and a wooden picnic table. I kill the motor but leave my keys in the ignition. On the horizon, a dark boil of smoke announces that the Rogues will have plenty of work tomorrow.

Getting out of the car, I cross to the picnic table, hop on top, and give the impressive drop-off a serious once over. Or pretend to. There might be more than a few stupid tears between me and the view because I've just been crashed by a pity party.

Behind me, gravel crunches as Pick pulls his bike off the road and coasts to a stop. Leather and denim rustles as he throws a leg over the seat and then approaches. For a big man, he moves quietly. He won't hesitate or pull his punch about what he saw back there in the camp. For some reason, that's not as scary as it should be. I think he might actually listen to my side of the story and not rush to judgment, and not just because a guy who looks like him and who rides around in leather on a bike has probably been on the wrong side of assumptions before. But because Pick's a fair man. Dirty, rough around the edges, and more than a little bull-headed when he gets an idea—but fair.

I might just freaking trust this man and I have no idea how that happened. Perhaps I should revisit my belief in Santa Claus and the Tooth Fairy as well.

"Hey," he says when he's standing in front of me, opening his arms wide. He's blocking the fabulous view, but that works for me. I stare at him instead. "You want to tell me what this is about? Why there's an officer of the law looking for you?"

Despite my newly discovered trust, I really don't want to answer that particular question. So... fight fire with fire, right? "Did you tell him about me?"

He smiles, real slow. "What do you think, Sarah Jo?"

"Do I look omniscient? If I knew, I wouldn't ask."

"No," he says. "Of course I didn't tell him anything. I was singularly unhelpful, as were the rest of the guys. We didn't know a damned thing. Had never spotted your pretty face before. By the way, Colt wants your number. Last I saw him, Deputy Douche was getting back in his car, as unenlightened as when he arrived."

Deputy Douche. I like that name. It sums up Thad's sterling qualities so well.

Pick gestures with his arms, another, smaller *Come here* gesture. "You gonna spill the details now?"

Not a chance. I wrap my arms around myself. If I need a hug, I can totally self-provide. My butt's staying planted right here on the picnic table at a safe distance from Mr. Hotshot. "Nope. Not a chance in hell."

"Uh-huh. That's what I figured. You have trust issues, Sarah Jo."

"Working on it," I snap. Wow. I might even mean it because some part of me I'd thought was long dead rears its head, almost begging for us to launch ourselves at this guy and spill all. Pick mutters something and drops his arms. Maybe they got tired, or maybe he just realized that hell would freeze over before I flew to him like some helpless little lady.

He covered for me, though, and that gets the warm fuzzies going. He hasn't asked too many questions. Has, in fact, simply followed my lead in a show of support that's as unexpected as it is appreciated. Pick is turning out to be far more than a dare or a delicious treat. He's rock solid and a genuine hero . . . but he's also alpha to his core. Taking control is second nature to him. I need to run hard—in the opposite direction. He's used to being in charge and giving orders. My deputy ex was like that, and I've totally learned my lesson there. No more take-charge authority figures for me. Never, ever again.

Pick does some more silent staring. Or maybe it's waiting. I'm tempted to stick my tongue out at him to break the growing tension, but there's something impossibly sweet about him. He came after me. Maybe he was worried. Maybe he *cared*. Hah. As if. It's far more likely that he just wants to finish what we started yesterday. I chew my lip and examine his face, looking for answers. The sexual tension between us is out of this world, but that's all we have going for us. One hot kiss and an even hotter twenty minutes in a supply cabin. He didn't even get an orgasm out of it, although I haven't heard him complaining.

Since I'm watching him like he's my favorite show, I know the exact moment he decides *screw this*. Moving slowly enough that I could dance away and make a joke, he steps up to the table and pulls me into his arms, hugging me close. And I let him. Are you surprised? Because it shocks the hell out of me. Worse, I turn and rub my cheek against his chest like I'm his goddamned sex kitten.

His voice rumbles overhead. "You change your mind, you know where to find me, honey. I got one question, though." He pauses, clearly waiting for some sign from me. But I'm obviously clueless, so I shut the hell up and eventually he continues. "Why did Deputy Douche come all the way up here looking for you? Seems like one hell of a drive."

"Six hours," I agree. Oops. This is why it's better to say nothing because I've just incriminated myself.

"So you do have a passing acquaintance with the good officer," he drawls.

Admit nothing. "I can read a map," I offer, shoving away from him. It's harder to do than I'd like. He feels so good, all steely muscles wrapped up in sun-warmed leather and cotton. Someone should totally bottle that. "And do math. That doesn't mean Thad came out here looking for me." I point toward the motorcycle parked alongside the road. "You should go back to fighting your fires."

Our moment—whatever it is—needs to be over.

Pick just smiles. "And you'll come back to cooking dinner in camp as soon as *Thad*'s gone?"

Shit. Well, it's not like it's really a secret that I've got secrets, is it? I'm still going for somewhat plausible deniability.

"Sure." I fold my arms over my chest, and wait for him to get a move on. Unfortunately, Pick's as stubborn as he is large. He leans down, placing his hands on either side of me. His fingers brush my hips, he's that close. I can't bring myself to complain.

"Here's the thing, honey," he says. "You can't cook worth shit. So I have to wonder why you came out here, in the middle of nowhere, providing three squares for a crew of hotshots."

I slap a hand on his chest and shove. God, he feels so warm and solid beneath the cotton T-shirt that proclaims BIG BEAR ROGUES. I so do *not* want to curl my fingers into that fabric and pull him closer. The man just insulted my cooking skills. I should be insulted—not turned on. "You heard about this little thing called the economy? It sucks."

"Uh-huh. Which is why you're on a first-name basis with Deputy Douche and hiding out on the road instead of starting dinner."

He knows my work schedule? I'm not sure if I'm flattered or creeped out that he's been watching me enough to know when I work.

"I'm a bad employee." He just insulted my cooking—he can hardly disagree.

"You work at camp, so you should know something." He doesn't move away. Doesn't give me the space I crave. He just keeps me boxed in... and I like it. He smells like laundry detergent and wood smoke, plus something indefinably, indescribably *Pick*. He's freaking spectacular, but he doesn't even seem to know it. He prowls through camp, putting everyone to rights, and he doesn't notice the feminine looks that follow his ripped and corded body. God, I'd like to get him into an actual bed. I'll bet he's the best, the kind of man who gives as well as gets and who ruins you for anyone else because he's hung and he sets the bar high.

"Hey." He nudges my cheek with his fingers. "Still

talking here. Earth to Sarah Jo."

"Present." God. Am I blushing? *Please say no.*

"You work here," he repeats, "and that makes you part of the team, okay? That means the Rogues have your back. Trouble follows you here, trouble has to deal with us. I sent Hill packing."

He got rid of Thad. Relief courses through me, and it turns out that all that adrenaline actually does make my knees weak. There's a funny, low-grade buzz throughout my body and a prickle of heated awareness in my belly and lower. Where Pick spent quality time yesterday. I can't tell if I'm just relieved or horribly turned on. I can go back to camp, and my nemesis won't be waiting for me there. The reprieve will be only temporary—Thad is stubborn—but, God, I appreciate it.

"Right. Trouble." The most pressing trouble I have right now is my reaction to this man. I kissed him and went up in flames. I don't need another chance at his mouth to know that the reality of Pick will be better than any fantasy I can dream up.

"Bottom line me," I suggest, tilting my head back. The move buys me a few inches, no more. Certainly not enough to defuse the six-plus feet of rugged charm pressed against me. "Are you offering to be my knight errant?"

He blinks, all delicious masculine confusion. He finally doesn't know what to say. Good. He doesn't get to have the upper hand here. I might be done with men, but confused Pick does something to my insides. Dazed suits him, and I love knocking him off balance.

Just to keep him off said balance, or so I tell myself, I run a hand down his chest, savoring the solid beat of his heart. That's my Pick, rock solid inside and out. He's dependable. Loyal to the core. He looks out for his team members, but I'm no hotshot. No matter what promises he makes, I don't really belong here. His fire camp is a temporary pit stop on my journey, and I'll move on sooner rather than later.

"You in the market?" he asks finally as my hands dip lower, resting against the rock-hard muscles of his abdomen. This is crazy. I blame him.

"No." I push gently and this time he backs up. Hopping down off the picnic table, I head back to my car. I don't need his help. Don't have to humble myself to accept it. I stand on my own two feet. Always.

"All right." He follows me and opens my door for me so I can slide into the driver's seat. "You headed back to camp?"

I hear the unspoken question: or am I hitting the road? His face watches mine patiently, focused and determined as he waits for me to answer.

"For now, yeah." Where else can I go, really? Back on the road, sure, but the paycheck, however small, is desperately needed, and running out on the girls seems wrong. Besides, I like to think that the girls in the Break Up Club and I are friends, so I'd have to stop and say goodbyes there, too.

"Good." He shuts my door. "Wouldn't be the same without you, and that's the truth."

Now it's my turn to be speechless. Does he... like me? What does that even mean? Rather than try to come up with something to say, I settle for driving off. Leaving Pick standing by the side of the road is unexpectedly difficult, and I regret every inch I put between us. I do it, though.

I'm not stupid.

That man's every bit as dangerous to my peace of mind as Thad Hill.

11

SARAH JO

I SHOULDN'T.

I really, really shouldn't.

I slipped away from Baby Bear Lodge as quietly as I could. Yes, I coasted down the driveway before starting the engine. I was in super sex ninja stealth mode. My fellow members of the Break Up Club would probably condone this little midnight field trip, but I'm not in the mood for their teasing. Not now. Somehow, what started as a camp game, a gentle tease, has grown into something more, but that *more* is between me and Pick. Just the two of us and no one else. I tried to figure out what it might be the entire drive from my cabin to camp, but answers eluded me.

Wrapped in sleep, the fire camp is dark and silent. Stars dot the night sky above, impossibly bright. I don't even need a flashlight to see where I'm going. Pick's RV is parked on the other side of camp, and the man inside draws me like a compass to magnetic north.

I don't know what I was thinking, coming here. I have no invitation, just this… chemistry. I'm not even sure I can deal with seeing Pick. He mixes me up inside, making me feel all these things. Lust, need, embarrassment, confusion, aggravation, more lust—it's a long list. Pick's like a bag of chips, and there's no way I stop until I'm licking the crumbs, still craving more. I can tell myself as many times as I want that I'll stop after one. One kiss, one touch, one night of hook up sex. One big fat lie. One certainly hasn't been enough for me so far.

So I get out of the car and make my way toward the RV. He hasn't even bothered locking it. The handle turns easily beneath my fingers.

PICK

I HAVE COMPANY. The door to my RV snicks open, light spilling in from the camp outside. It's still dark as fuck, though, so I'm not certain who's making free with my place. I lever myself up on one arm. Late-night visits aren't usually social calls, and the red numbers on the alarm clock read well after one o'clock. My boys do like their practical jokes, though, so I pull a wait-and-see.

It's Christmas.

Santa dropped the biggest, best-ever gift on my doorstop and I can't wait to unwrap it. *Her*.

Because that's Sarah Jo inching her way inside my door. Her oversized Hanes is rendered semi-transparent by the faint light behind her, exposing the curve of her waist, and Christ, her magnificent tits. I didn't pay nearly enough attention to those tits when I had her spread out on that desk, and that's a mistake I should fix ASAP.

"You need something, Sarah Jo?"

She hovers in the open doorway, rubbing one foot against the other. One *bare* foot against the other. I hope she dropped her shoes at the door, but I get the feeling she drove up here this way. I should take a look at her feet. The ground outside is rough. We've got sticks, pinecones, and a shitload of stones. She could be cut up. I should make sure she's okay, offer to kiss it better wherever it hurts.

"I've changed my mind." Her voice is low but sure. "If your offer still stands."

Logically, I know she's wearing a pair of denim shorts beneath that gigantic cotton shroud, but it's no good. I should get up and take a cold shower. Or find me a nice mountain stream to soak in until I can think about something, anything, other than putting her in my bed and making her come. Again. Doing what I should do is a goddamn problem. I want this woman something fierce.

I find myself gaping like a hooked fish, my dick tenting the sheet over my lap. Hope to fuck Sarah Jo has really poor night vision, or she's gonna think I'm making assumptions about what her presence in my RV means. At dark o'clock. Mostly naked.

She slams the door shut, pads forward, and stumbles over my gear bag. Guess that answers the question of how good her night vision is. She seems to be flying blind here, which makes two of us. I'm used to the dark, however, so I can see the way she holds her hands out in front of her, sort of feeling her way. I reach out and hook a finger in the hem of her T-shirt, tugging her in my direction.

"One o'clock and two feet," I promise her.

She lets me guide her, moving forward slowly until she bumps against my bed. Should have gone to her, right? I have no idea what's happening next, but I know I don't want to hop out of bed wearing nothing but a pair of boxers, sporting a monster hard-on and a grin.

She plants a knee on the bed. "You promised you'd always have a pair of open arms for me."

"Uh-huh." Fuck me if anything more coherent is coming out of my mouth tonight. Her eyes roam over my face, looking for something, and I try to slap an expression on my face that's more welcoming than ravening beast, but I totally want to eat her up. A small smile tugs at the corner of her mouth. Okay. She seems to like what she sees, so that's good.

Just to test that hypothesis, and not because I'm dying to touch her (*liar*), I wrap my hand around her knee, urging her forward. Sure enough, beneath that too-big T-shirt, she's all long, bare legs wherever I touch. Those have to be the shortest shorts in all creation, and I'm a fan.

"I'll take that as a *yes*." She grins and shimmies out

of her shorts. My head and my dick vie to see which will explode first, but before I can decide, she's swings a leg over me, straddling me until we're face-to-face. My head (one guess as to which one) promptly engages in a little mathematical exercise and determines that there are exactly three things standing between my dick and her pussy. One sheet, one pair of boxers, her panties. And a few scruples. I should get busy removing those, right?

The scruples, not the panties.

Or maybe I *do* mean the other way round.

"This is unexpected. But good." I put my hands on her waist. That's nice, neutral territory. Better than palming her tits or asking if she'd mind if I ate her pussy for my midnight snack.

"Make it better," she demands, and I bite back a smile. She's so take-charge. It's downright adorable. Since I want what she wants, however, there's no problem. I tug the T-shirt up and she helps me, grabbing the hem and yanking. Okay. So we might not want *exactly* the same things. She's clearly in a rush—again—and I'm in the mood to take my time. Since I'm bigger and stronger, I end up in control of the T-shirt ascent, exposing her body in a slow, sexy striptease in the night-lit RV. First, her panties. Some kind of silky purple material this time, with little white polka dots and thin ribbons crisscrossing her hips. They're pretty fucking amazing, although the woman in them is even better.

Then she treats me to the soft curve of her belly and higher as the T-shirt clears her shoulders and disappears over her head. Her breasts are goddamned beautiful, perfect handfuls, the nipples a sweet dark rose. I'd look all night if she'd let me, but she swings the shirt over her head and lets it fly. It disappears somewhere into the shadows and good fucking riddance. She doesn't need to cover up around me. She makes a face, hands flying to her hair to pat and smooth. She's tousled, but I'm just going to mess her up even more.

Where to start? She's pretty much riding my dick through the sheet. It reminds me of how fast and hard we went at in the storage cache. She loved it when I ate her pussy, and I absolutely want to do that again, but I want other things, too. I can't stop thinking about what I haven't had a chance to do yet. Like fuck her gorgeous tits. Lick and suck those pretty nipples and see if she can come that way for me, too. I run my hands up her sides and palm her breasts, working my fingers over those delicious curves.

"Come here." Pretty sure my voice comes out more

growl than request, but I'm hungry for her mouth too, and feeling greedy. She leans right into me, onboard with my new plan.

"Mmmm," she whimpers. "Definitely better."

Playful Sarah Jo is fucking amazing. She's not too quiet, either—I'm gonna catch hell from my teammates tomorrow but she won't get any complaints from me. She can come riding my face, my dick, my fingers and scream that news to the entire camp if that's what makes her happy. Fuck, not as if I don't love everything about her. She's stubborn and mischievous to a fault, but I look at her and all I see is Sarah Jo. I'm counting my lucky stars that she came to me tonight, so whatever she wants, it's hers.

She may be basically dry-fucking my dick, but our kiss starts out surprisingly sweet. Mouths closed, lips on lips while I give into temptation and finger her nipples as I take her mouth. She rocks gently against me and then harder, the sexy roll of her hips picking up speed as she breathes harder. She's practically panting when she pulls back from our kiss.

"You going to undress for me?" She doesn't stop riding me so I'm not sure how she expects a coherent answer. My dick has plenty of things to say for me, as it's pointing out.

"You taking these off?" I counter her question with an important one of my own, hooking a thumb in the ribbons at the sides of her panties and tugging.

Her eyes darken. "I could be convinced."

She slides off me, taking her sweet time to do so. When she stands up on the bed, her head almost brushes the RV's roof. We don't have a whole lot of room to work with here. I settle back and enjoy my new view as she slowly works those panties down her hips, over that sweet pussy and her thighs, before stepping out of them. Fuck me, but she's killing me. The kick that sends those panties over the side of the bed, though, is pure impatience.

I take advantage of the moment to shove my boxers and the sheet down, looking my fill all the while. I'm putting my tongue right there, I decide, where I can see the dark shadow of hair between her thighs. I'll be all over her, kissing and licking until she hollers and we set my RV to rocking something fierce. I don't know what I've done to deserve this, but she's apparently decided to green-light my fantasies for the night, and I don't need asking twice.

"Shoot." She sort of hops in place, which makes her

tits bounce and I might be drooling. "The condom was in my shorts."

It's good that she's come prepared, but I've got her covered. I'd never put her at risk. I slide open the bedside table drawer and fish out a foil square. I'm not even sure why I have these since the only action I've seen in months is fire action, but thank Christ anyhow. Her eyes follow my hands as I tear open the package and roll the latex down.

"Come on back?" I manage to make it a fucking question. Unless I miss my guess, my Sarah Jo likes being the one in charge, and I can work with that tonight. I lie back, head on the pillows. Besides, damned if it isn't sexy, waiting for her to ravish me. I can certainly let her take charge once in a while. Her smile echoes mine, so game on.

She straddles me, cradling my dick right where he wants to be in the hot, wet valley between her thighs. When she leans forward to kiss me again, I slip inside her hot, sweet slit just the tiniest amount. She gasps. I groan. It's the fucking best symphony ever, but we're playing allegro when I'd planned on lento. I'll just have to save the slow, long ride for later. We've got hours before the sun comes up and the camp gets busy.

Hot and fast now.

Slow and sweet later.

Her kiss grows hotter, more desperate, her mouth devouring mine as her tongue sweeps inside. I cup her breasts, thumbing the rosy tips. She returns the favor, her fingers finding my nipples and pinching erotically. She gives as good as she gets, my Sarah Jo.

She tears her mouth from mine. "You like that?"

Fuck yes, I do.

"Just as much as you like my touching those pretty breasts."

"So we're square." Smiling impishly, she lifts up, sinks down, and does her best to take goddamned all of me in one fast move. Uh-uh. She doesn't get to rush the ending. Putting my hands on her hips, I control her descent, matching it with my ascent, pushing in, giving her what we both want.

If it were possible to fuck ourselves to death, we'd be giving it a fair shot. The bed creaks, protesting each move we make. She takes me, her fingers digging into my shoulders as she works herself on my dick like it's her own personal toy. And I… lose it. Lose control, lose myself in the hot, sweet wildness that is Sarah Jo. She rides me like a rodeo queen, rising up fast and slamming down hard. She drives me out of my mind, and she knows it. She watches me fiercely, gauging my pleasure. I'd bet my last dollar my Sarah Jo knows exactly how close I am to coming. That's good, I have no complaints, but I'm not the only one in this bed, am I? This has to be even better for her. So I take control, flipping her over and pinning her to the bed beneath me.

I slam into her, long, luxurious, powerful strokes, seating myself deep inside her body. She's small, I'm large, but somehow we fit together just right. She whimpers, fingers clutching at my shoulders, leaving red crescents.

"Don't you dare stop," she whisper-yells into my ear, biting down hard on the lobe. I grunt and hammer into her as her hips push up against mine, seeking an even deeper penetration, and I grab her ass with both hands and lift her. Stroke deeper and slower, then pull back and drive inside her again.

Yeah. Right *there*. I adjust and seat myself again, drinking in her little groans and breathy whimpers. Her fingers push and pull as she strives for the climax hovering just out of reach.

Dropping a hand between us, I find her clit and pinch.

"Let go for me, honey." My next stroke forces the palm of my hand hard against the top of her pussy and she stiffens, legs quivering. Her body comes around mine, and that's my green light. I go over the edge right behind.

PICK

TWO HOURS after she bangs me into happy oblivion, Sarah Jo sneaks away. Or attempts to. Since we fell asleep naked and tangled up together, she's facing a logistical challenge if she wants to make a getaway, and clearly she doesn't want to go panty-less. After she wriggles out from beneath my arm, she sort of ninja-crawls across the floor, sweeping around for her clothes. I'd like to point out that some shit gets easier if you turn the lights on, but Sarah Jo's a big fan of hiding. She might actually have a coronary if I shone a light anywhere near her. So I enjoy the show she's giving me. Fucking sucks she's about to cover up that fantastic ass, although not as much as her need to leave me alone and in the dark does. I consider letting her know I'm awake and that she doesn't need to sneak.

Yeah. Don't think that would go well, and I won't stop her if she wants to leave. I'm not fooling myself, either. Sarah Jo's not worried about the rest of the camp learning that we've hooked up. Sure, we'll come in for some teasing, but the Rogues won't push too far. Not once I make it clear that Sarah Jo's feelings matter.

And when the fuck did that happen? She invited herself over. We should be firmly in hook up territory, and her leaving shouldn't come as any kind of surprise. I've been pretending I'm down with whatever she wants, but the truth is that I'd like more. I'm ready to all Oliver Twist on her cute ass and ask for some more, please. And it's not just the sex, although she's amazing and I'd never want to go without sex. It's that she *matters* to me. You know how you hit the grocery and you get flour, eggs, and a bag of other crap that you line up on the kitchen counter? By themselves, that shit's just groceries. Mix it all together, however, and you've got cake and that's something out of the ordinary. Sarah Jo's my triple-layer fudge, my red velvet goodness, a cupcake with mile-high frosting and a hell of a lot of substance underneath all that sweet. I like her. Okay. Fuck that. I more than like her. She's snuck up on my heart, and boom, there she is, front and center in everything I'm doing and thinking.

This is not a great state of events seeing as how she clearly doesn't feel the same way. My big clue? The way she's sneaking out of my place before the sun comes up and I can get a cup of coffee into her because she doesn't want to say anything. *Good morning* is apparently too complicated for her, which is too damned bad. I have plenty of things to say to her.

She steals my T-shirt and shimmies into her shorts bare-assed. There's some muttering, a jingle of keys, and then the door opens with a quiet snick; a flash of night sky fading fast into dawn, and she's gone.

"Bye," I say to the empty RV.

Fucking sucks. I roll over and punch the pillow.

I've never been in a hurry to settle down or marry up—but I've generally avoided one-night stands, too. I've never been a fan of sticking my dick anywhere with frequent flyer miles because I'm a special fucking snowflake about feeling special. I like my girl to know who I am, and I like to know her. If you can't have a conversation with someone wearing clothes, how are you gonna do any better naked? So maybe I haven't always had love, but I've definitely had like. Nothing about Sarah Jo screams *permanent* or *keep me*. She's a temporary fire camp hire who's made her intentions of moving on after the summer all too clear. So if quickie sex isn't what I want—and my dick points out that parts of us are way okay with it—Sarah Jo should have been off-limits. Over and done with. No thinking about her, pining after her, or trying to get her into bed. I can't have it in my mind that it'll happen again.

Yeah. Right.

Non-naked talking isn't on Sarah Jo's to do list. We won't be having long conversations about our favorite fucking movies or taking romantic walks by the lake. Not that that's all bad because a mountain lake is freezing cold even in July, and I like my balls non-shriveled, thank you very much. No talking. No getting to know her. No anything. But some things don't need words. Have you ever noticed that? So while I wait for her to come round and open up, I'll just have to keep an eye out and watch over her some. And if that sounds stalkerish, just give me credit for having good intentions. Just watching her is a joy. Her laugh lights up a room. And trouble is definitely riding her ass.

So what if she doesn't trust me? I text her to see if she's gotten home okay. She doesn't answer, but that's okay. Texting and driving isn't safe, and I want her safe.

And happy. Happy's good, too. Then I get up. I'll go for a run because no way I go back to sleep now, and trust me, being a hotshot requires you to stay in peak shape. Somedays, hauling gear from point A to point B feels like trying to drag a cannon uphill in the grass.

By the time I'm lacing my sneakers and it's gray outside rather than pitch black, Sarah Jo hasn't text back and I know she has to be home. Unless she ran out of gas or that POS car of hers crapped out and she's stranded by the roadside. I should totally check on that. I text again.

```
If you don't prove you're okay, I'm
coming out for a welfare check.
```

Then I grab my earbuds and head outside. I'm debating between hitting the trail or hitting the highway when she finally texts back. She doesn't waste any words on me, either. She just sends a picture. Of herself.

She's in bed. Do you think that's an invitation? Because I'd love to take it that way. Plus, she's still wearing my shirt and my inner caveman demands I beat on my chest. Do some growling. Possibly tattoo *Pick's* on her ass or mark her with my jizz. Too much? The thing is, I'm not sure I'll ever get enough of her.

> You stole my shirt.

Think she might have stolen something else, but I'm not going there. Not yet. Not like I was doing much with my heart anyhow. She kissed me. She rode my big dick like a pogo stick and rode the hell out of me, but she doesn't trust me. No matter how awesome the sex is, she doesn't like losing control. I get that. From our first kiss to when she opened my door and came straight on over to my bed, she's taken charge and she's never really let go.

Does it sound like I'm a whiney bitch to complain about her take-charge attitude in bed? Because it's not that I didn't love fucking her and being fucked by her. I loved it. Think all the moaning and groaning I did proved that. It's just that she's busy taking charge because then she can keep me out of the important parts of her. And I don't know how to fix that, because although I enjoyed the hell out of our night together, I do want more than acrobatics and a mind-blowing orgasm that still has me seeing stars and tenting the front of my running shorts.

PICK

SARAH JO, me, and a Saturday night. If I want to be more than her midnight hook up, I need to make a move. And this way I get a two-for-one.

I show her a good time, treat her like a queen, and let the whole world—*my* world—see that we're together and not just making my RV rock. This is the civilized version of jizzing on her tits and inviting everyone to look at what I've done. When I pull my bike into the parking lot of *Drink Up,* I'm congratulating myself on my genius. Since I picked Sarah Jo up at her place and we rode here together, I've had her arms wrapped around me, hugging me. Holding me close. For fucking *miles.*

Tell me that's not genius.

She pops off my bike, balancing herself with a hand

on my shoulder as she shucks the helmet I bought for her. I like the way she leans on me, the way she's letting me take care of her. Not like she can't do for herself, but it's that caveman of mine. He wants to beat his chest and bring down a mastodon and BBQ its ass for her.

She grins at me. "It's not the titty bar. You think you'll survive?"

Fuck, I love the way she laughs, the giggle-snort that starts somewhere near her belly and just flies out her mouth. And I love that we're starting to have couple jokes, a history. Pretty soon I'll fucking be calling her *bunny* and I'll be a *boo*.

"I'm taking a rain check," I say, saluting her.

She laughs and tugs on my hand. "Come on, or your friends will drink the place dry."

It's a distinct possibility. *Drink Up* is beery, dark, and absolutely rocking. The décor is mostly neon beer sign and dust, with a side of old, bad paneling and vinyl seating. Some of my boys are already doing the conga on the small dance floor, shaking their asses to the country music belting out of the antiquated jukebox. I hacked that shit once, made it play Handel's *Messiah* at top volume. Colt and I waltzed. It was an epic night, but I sense tonight will be even better.

"Beer?" I grin at my soon-to-be-girl. This hotshot has a plan.

She beams back at me. "And if I say no?"

"Got water. Might have pop." I drop a kiss on her nose and amble toward the bar. *Drink Up* is famous (or notorious) for its lack of variety. Your choices are beer—or beer. Regular or light. On a good day, it comes in a bottle.

"Beer," she says mock-solemnly. "Would be lovely."

Sarah Jo tags along behind me, her fingers tucked into the back of my belt. Her fingertips brush the sensitive spot at the top of my ass, and I think she knows exactly what she's doing to me. She keeps it up, I'm gonna ink her name right there.

Lola's already present, holding court in a corner booth. She alternates between shouting with laughter and working her phone. Think she must have misplaced Hunter because he's just about the only hotshot not here. By the time I have our beers, Olivia's dragged Lola out onto the dance floor. Lola's skirt is so short that I'm ready to take bets on a wardrobe malfunction.

Sarah Jo's a little more covered up, which shouldn't surprise anyone. In deference to the whole Saturday-night and ride-on-my-bike thing, she's wriggled into a pair of jeans that hug her ass and her legs before flaring out around her ankles into some kind of embroidered thing that almost cover her cowboy boots. The top probably has some kind of name, but let's just call it gorgeous. It ties around her neck and then skims her tits before flaring out like a tent or a pretty white cloud or some poetic shit. When she moves, she flashes me hints of her stomach and waist, so I'm definitely a fan. I sit myself down in a corner booth and pull her onto my lap. This way I can hold her close and make room for other people. I'm a total fucking Boy Scout.

Out on the floor, Lola launches into a wild, arm-swinging, hip-rocking dance. Her ponytail threatens a couple of nearby hotshots with whiplash, but she looks happy. Her short denim skirt bounces up and down, the ruffles on her red-and-white polka dot blouse taking flight. It's fucking mesmerizing.

"You need a shirt like that." The din in *Drink Up* has achieved deafening levels, so I whisper the words into her ear because communication's important in a relationship. As punctuation on that sentence, I nip her ear. Gently because my caveman's still out in the parking lot. Don't worry. He'll catch up.

A grin lights up Sarah Jo's face. "You like it?"

"Yours is better."

That goes for everything about Sarah Jo. Fucking lucky Hunter didn't figure that out for himself and try to take my girl. Sarah Jo wriggles around on my lap like she's trying to get comfortable. Probably should lend her a hand since it's my dick that's spearing her in the ass in an excellent imitation of an iron bar. On the other hand, since it's her fault that I'm currently in this condition…

She wriggles some more and I bite back a groan.

"Is that for me?"

"Always."

I mean it too.

All these feelings are new. They distract me. And that is why I don't realize that Sarah Jo's up to something until her hand squeezes my dick through my jeans.

"I don't like to share," she says as if we're talking about a beer or an order of fries.

"There's plenty of me to go around." She squeezes, her hand working dirty, dirty magic on me, and I growl. "But no sharing."

"All mine." A smile curves her mouth. She twists her head so she can see my face, and I can't stop touching her, too. I'm running my hands up her thighs, over her waist, just barely staying out of triple-X filthy territory. Sarah Jo's spent the summer hiding in plain sight, so I don't think she wants to get arrested for public indecency now.

She cups the back of my head with one hand, shutting me up with her mouth. And I'm not complaining. I kiss her back, my hands going wild, pulling her closer, tugging at every dirty, fabulous, amazing inch of my Sarah Jo. Fucking gonna come in a corner booth at a dive bar, and I love it. I love…

Nope. Not going there.

A whoop from the dance floor breaks up our kiss. Sarah Jo jumps like she's forgotten we're not alone in bed. She instinctively turns her attention back to the dance floor, and I watch with her.

Buttoned up, starchy, rule-following Olivia shocks the heck out of me. Pretty sure she also gives the bar a collective heart attack as she launches into a slow, dirty grind, working her ass in her neat pencil skirt. When she drags her fingers down the front of her blouse, tongues start hanging out. She's gorgeous and happy and ten bucks says one of my teammates makes a move on her tonight.

Sarah Jo bounces off my lap with enough vigor that I grunt. I've got plans for my balls and my dick later tonight, but she's oblivious to using them as a launching pad. I'll let her kiss everything better when we're alone.

She's practically vibrating. "Dance with me."

I'm built like a bear, not Baryshnikov. I glance around the bar, taking in the guys crowding the space. Most of them are a little rough around the edges, a jeans-wearing, T-shirt-sporting crew. A lot of them are built because you don't dig line for eight hours a day and not gain muscle. A few are wearing shirts with actual buttons and something besides steel-toed boots. Fucking Colt looks like Mr. GQ in something that even I know cost the sun, moon, and a half-dozen pricey constellations. The man is not a cheap date.

None of us, however, are wearing tutus. Or dancing shoes.

"I don't dance." I hang onto my beer like it's gonna anchor me to our booth. "Come back over here and let me kiss you some more."

I watch as she makes this twisty-face with her mouth, thinking about my offer. The jukebox segues into something slow and extra achy-breaky-heartish and the dance floor rapidly empties out except for Lola and

Olivia semi-groping and grinding. Colt commandeers the waitress; Adrian produces a little blonde from somewhere and they start making tidy, awkward circles in place on the dance floor.

"Dance," Sarah Jo decides. She waggles her fingers at me.

I look down. I'm still not wearing a tutu.

I can't remember the last time I danced for anything other than a joke. My waltz with Colt, a drunken conga line with my boys—these things were just for fun and some laughs. It's not that I don't fucking love music or that I mind getting up in front of a crowd; it's that my body never got the rhythm memo. I can't dance for shit.

"I don't dance," I repeat.

Sarah Jo tugs the empty beer out of my hand and sets it on the table. "Can't or won't?"

"Both," I grumble.

She waves her hand in the air. "You don't have to be good at it. Just look at Lola."

Lola has tits to distract the rest of the bar, plus I don't really care what she thinks. Sarah Jo is different. I'd rather not make a public display of my inadequacies.

But she's sneaking wistful looks at the dance floor and the song has to be half fucking over, right? If she wants to do this, I'll just have to man up and hope it doesn't go too badly.

"Come on." I stand up, grabbing her hand and towing her after me. She doesn't hesitate. She follows my lead, and I find myself pressed against her curvy body as we gyrate stiffly in place. I have no idea what she thought we'd do out here, but I wrap my arms around her loosely, tucking my hands on the top of her ass, and breathe her in. She smells so fucking good, like a strawberry Sarah Jo piña colada, and I'm buzzing on just her. Doesn't help my dancing any, but I like it.

Sarah Jo slides her arms around me, her fingertips toying with the hem of my T-shirt and making little raids on the skin beneath. My only plan was to get her out here and make her happy. She rests her head against my chest, exhales, and then she just kind of melts into the music. She's fucking gorgeous, swaying, and dipping, and lighting up the floor. Me? Not so much. I step awkwardly from foot to foot like some kind of bear-loon hybrid. Colt actually winces as he slowly two-steps around us.

Fuck that noise. Because Sarah Jo's smiling at me, happiness and amusement lighting up her eyes, and I don't think she minds that I'm shit in the dancing department. She moves her hips slowly to the music, her top bouncing and floating and generally driving me crazy because I know how easy it would be to get my hands underneath it again and pet her tits more.

This is when Hunter shows up and sets off a cataclysmic chain reaction. Lola spots him, her face lighting up.

Sarah Jo shifts nervously. "I think I need to stage an intervention."

But it's too late.

Lola's pretty fucking unstoppable. Under other circumstances, she'd make an awesome hotshot. She heads straight for Hunter, breaking stride just once to grab a beer from the tray of a passing waitress. Maybe she's thirsty? Fuck if I know what she's doing. Lola chugs her stolen booty and tears off the tab. Her belch is loud enough that I hear it over all of the goddamned country music. And then she rubs the stupid purple rabbit's foot hanging off her purse and makes for Hunter.

I've spent hundreds of hours with the man. I've had his back, and he's had mine. You learn a few things about danger when it's you, Mother Nature, and a shit-ton of flames. You learn to trust your instincts, when to advance, and when to back the hell up and retreat. Hunter needs to run. Instead, the idiot stands there and smiles as Lola charges toward him. He's in the hot zone with the mother of all fires coming for him and he doesn't seem to realize it.

She leans into him.

They kiss (Sarah Jo and I do it much better).

She drops to her knees.

Sarah Jo curses and starts steering us toward the happy couple. "She's all in."

I'll admit it. My first thought? That Lola's about to deliver a world-class blow job right here, right now. Her mouth's on the level of Hunter's dick, and while there are things I'm happy to watch on the big screen, there are also things I don't want to see in real life.

"What is she doing?"

I sound like an idiot, but Lola can't be doing this, can she?

"It's so romantic."

Does Sarah Jo sound… wistful?

"Hunter Black." Lola holds up the beer can tab. "Will you marry me?"

"No," I say before my brain catches up with my mouth.

Hunter looks stunned. He didn't see this coming. Weeks of hanging around Lola, and she still manages to surprise him. He blinks at her, hands opening and closing by his side. She could be explaining quantum physics in Hindu for all he gets it. *Drink Up* holds its collective breath. Well, all except Colt, who yells out something congratulatory. Hunter looks like he just got brained by a falling snag.

Maybe the good folks in charge of the forestry department are fucking with us. Maybe we're on one of those reality TV shows that sends in hidden cameras and then stages some drama. Because naturally this is the moment a gorgeous woman in a short, tight, black cocktail dress marches into the bar and right up to Hunter, and shit gets weird. Because that's his ex.

The woman who couldn't dump his ass fast enough.

The woman who sure looks like she's entertaining some hotshot-sized regrets—and itching to rumble with Lola.

And rather than take Lola's side, Hunter just makes it worse. Not only does he deny an engagement with Lola, but he tells her to stop being so dramatic. As if all this—her feelings, her proposal, her sharing air space with the ex—is *her* fault. As if it's not what he wants. At all.

"Way to fuck things up," I observe.

Lola must agree because a few painful, loud seconds later she gives Hunter the bird and runs out of the bar.

14

SARAH JO

SATURDAY NIGHT is date night. Pick lays down the law, going all gruff and stern on me. Pick insists we date. Okay. So he claims it's a hostage exchange and that he plans to swap my panties for his T-shirt. Yes, I slunk away from his RV panty-less. Apparently, he did some housecleaning after I left, and now said AWOL panties are in his possession. As long as he doesn't fly them from the roof of the RV or run them up the camp's flagpole, I'll live.

This dating business is why I find myself in town

and not in my cabin or hanging out with my Break Up Club girls. The Big Bear Rogues have tonight off, and they're crammed into *Drink Up,* Big Bear's one bar, swapping war stories and bad jokes. The guys are smoky, tired—and exhilarated. An honest-to-God jukebox belts out country tunes, and some super energetic dancing is reflected in the big glass mirror behind the bar. I've already line-danced with several smoke jumpers and at least half the Rogues. When Colt approaches me, hands out, I beg off. There's no way I dance another step until I've had a beer—and possibly an entire pitcher of water. I collapse, flushed and laughing, at our table.

Pick grins at me. He doesn't seem to mind my dancing with his teammates. I mean, it's not like I'm suggesting we have group sex right here on the dance floor, but it's a refreshing change to hang out with a guy who trusts me to respect the boundaries we've laid down. Thad always acted like I'd turn into Super Ho if he turned his back for even a second.

Pick claims he's not much of a dancer, but he led me out for that one turn at the beginning of the night, and then he did it a second time, after all the drama with Lola and Hunter went down. Pick's strong hands guided me down the line, and then he watched with a smile on his face as the other men twirled me enthusiastically. Honestly? None of them can dance for shit. It's more like happy stomping, but I guess I shouldn't have expected Fred Astaire to be putting out forest fires.

The fresh air that hits me when we finally leave the bar sometime well after midnight is a welcome wake-up call. It's been a weird night, but a good one (at least for everyone but Lola). The gravel parking lot is still plenty full of cars and beat-up trucks that reflect the vivid colors of the neon beer signs in the bar's window. I'm tipsy. Again, something I don't do. Drunk girls aren't in control girls. I suck in cool air, putting a hand on Pick's arm to steady myself. Heels are also a mistake tonight.

"You okay?" His amused laughter floats over my head. "I got you."

Does he? I guess he does.

"I'm worried about Lola," I announce to the rows of cars. It's true. She's not answering her phone, and Olivia says she's not at the cabins. I think she needs us, or needs some moral support and someone to tell her just how much of an asshole Hunter is. For a moment, though, I concentrate on just breathing, in and then out. I'm not, I tell myself, enjoying the feel of Pick's rock-hard muscles beneath my hand. I'm not copping a bonus feel of what I saw naked the other night. Nope. That's not why I'm standing here in the parking lot at all. I'm just getting my head on straight, clearing my mind before I do something insanely, publicly stupid like Lola.

Nothing more.

Unfortunately, no amount of fresh air or breathing time seems to undo the effect my hotshot has on me. His concern is seductive. And although I've stood on my own two feet for years, I know that in no way is he suggesting that I'm not capable. He's simply offering to help. Letting me know that he has my back, no strings attached.

The 64-thousand-dollar question is why.

It's not that I'm not feeling it. *Him.* Us. Sure, we had an amazing hook up, but we've managed to share air space at camp this week without ripping each other's clothes off. There have been looks, and I've been tempted. It turns out that Pick is a dirty texter. He's full of "thoughtful" suggestions for ways he can make me feel better. He convinced me to FaceTime the other night and let's just say the man talked me through an amazing orgasm. And yet I have a feeling that he's not just interested in having more in-person sex with me. It's ridiculous, right? He may have had his face buried in my hoohah—twice—but he barely knows me. I, on the other hand, have had enough relationships in my twenty-five years to know that the secrets I'm keeping are deal breakers. I screwed up badly, while Pick is a man who does everything the right way. He's a bona fide hero who goes out to battle wildland fires every day of the summer.

He wouldn't really want a woman like me.

Not if he knew.

We reach his bike before I can figure out if I really want to tell him and spoil this. Whatever this is. Staying silent isn't a great idea, but neither is confession. I'm not sure what to do, but then my past picks this moment to step out from between two parked trucks.

Thad Hill looks every bit as determined and confident as I remember him being. He also looks extremely pissed as he moves forward and blocks our path. No end run around him, even if I had somewhere to run. I've all but gone to the ends of the earth, and he can't let me go?

"Thad." My lips are dry and stick to my teeth, but I get his name out.

"Sarah Jo." His hands shift to his hips and the black utility belt there. For a heart-stopping moment, his fingers brush over the gun in its holster before he reaches for the cuffs. Would he actually kill me? I've never worried about that before—there are so many other ways to be at his mercy. The soft clink as he pulls the cuffs free almost gets lost in the sounds of doors slamming and men calling good-byes. "You're under arrest."

Thad takes another step forward, but then Pick's somehow between us. He moves quickly for a big man, fast and silent. As the two men lock eyes in a silent stare-down, I become aware of the other men in the parking lot closing in.

I've dreaded this moment for so long that it's almost anticlimactic. Thad wins. I lose. There's nowhere left to run unless I can somehow board a plane to Bora Bora and throw myself on the mercy of the Tahitians. It's almost a relief to know that the worst has happened. He'll put me in the back of his car, and, if I'm lucky, he'll settle for simply running me in to the station. The station that's at least a six-hour drive from here. I'm not thinking about the worst-case scenario—the one that involves me, the cuffs, and the backseat of Thad's car.

He's hinted more than once that I have some making up to do, and that I'd be starting on my knees.

"You got a warrant for that arrest?" Pick growls.

Someone else—Colt—steps up next to Pick. Now I've got a hotshot wall between me and Thad. When we danced earlier, Colt was a shameless flirt. Now he looks lethally mean. The two men make an impressive wall of shoulders, four hundred pounds of pure muscle and all on my side.

"What are the charges?" Colt adds his own question, the note of skepticism in his voice overt.

"Arson. And theft." Thad tries to advance. Maybe he expects Pick and Colt to back down or pull a Red Sea and open up a passage straight to me. They don't. I blink. Hard. I'm supposed to be handling this. Instead, they're handling Thad for me. He isn't their problem, though. I can do whatever I have to do.

"Pick . . ." That's my hand on his back. I don't remember putting it there. Even through the cotton T-shirt, I can feel the heat of him and the way the muscles in his back flex as he crosses his arms, sending Thad one of those silent male messages. Probably telegraphing *mine*. There's silence for a minute as Thad digests their opposition to his plans for me.

"You want to go with him?" Pick asks the question without turning his head.

"Not particularly," I admit, "but—"

"You got a warrant?" He addresses Thad again.

Thad blusters a bit and then starts spouting excuses. "On me? No. But Sarah Jo's got some answering to do. I'm running her in."

He sounds like a cross between a pissed-off parent and… I don't know what. But he's in his uniform, a small arsenal hanging off his belt. He's bigger than me, stronger, and he has a serious issue with my attempting to blow the whistle on what went down with Mrs. Joan. I know this is supposed to be the moment when I turn into some kind of caped crusader, eager to see justice done and scream my story to the world, but I'm a realist. Thad is a deputy sheriff, and I'm not. He has a sterling reputation, and I'm a little tarnished. There's zero reason for anyone to believe him over me, and I'd rather not pick a fight I can't win. Arguing with him isn't a great idea.

Apparently, I'm the only one who thinks this, however.

"No." Pick doesn't waste words.

Pick, of course, loves confrontation. I'm sure it has

something to do with the whole hotshot thing. If he were the kind of guy who preferred to hang back and watch shit happen, he'd make a terrible firefighter. I've seen enough of what they do to know that not only do the hotshots happily launch themselves into the middle of do-or-die situations, but they come out on top. They don't hesitate, and they win. There's probably a lesson in that for me, but I can't help but notice that most of them end up singed a little at one point or another.

"You stopping me?" This time, Thad's hand goes straight to his gun. He keeps the piece holstered, but the threat is unmistakable. He'd actually shoot Pick for standing in the way, and *that* is why I've spent so much time running instead of standing my ground.

My body and my head are in full agreement, too. The world goes icy cold, my vision narrowing to a cold, dark tunnel that drills in on the source of my current unhappiness. *Thad*. I'm not supposed to let him scare me like this, but he's unmistakably in charge. He has a gun, for God's sake. What else am I supposed to do?

Pick knows, of course. In fact, he's already talking.

"You produce a warrant, you can take Sarah Jo with you. Until then, I figure she decides when she goes and when she stays."

Around me, the other hotshots and jumpers nod, all on the same page as Pick. Thad curses (which is entirely unprofessional and deeply satisfying), clearly weighing the odds of shooting Pick and getting away with it. I think this may be the first time in a long time that he hasn't been able to bully his way to what he wants. Fortunately, he's also a coward, which is something I should have realized earlier. His hand slides away from the gun.

"I'll get the warrant," he threatens, fingers tapping his belt. "I'll be back. Don't run, Sarah Jo. Don't make me chase you again."

Have I mentioned that when I'm nervous, I tend to indulge in inappropriate humor? I'm the girl who giggles when she's sad or scared, too, so what happens next really shouldn't come as a surprise. Despite my panty-pissing terror, I flip Thad a jaunty, two-fingered salute because that's the perfect cover up for my insides, which are doing an excellent imitation of Jello. Someone laughs and Thad gets back into his car, closing the door far harder than is strictly necessary. I guess he feels he has a point to make. Seconds later, the car peels out of the parking lot, spitting gravel.

Mission accomplished, the other men slowly drift

away, truck doors slamming.

"You ready to head on back to camp?" Pick keeps his gaze steady on mine. He doesn't look pissed, or disappointed, or even curious. He just looks like he did yesterday. He looks like Pick.

I suck in one breath. Two. "You're taking my word over his?"

"Of course." He straddles his bike and offers me a helmet. Here we go. Once he has me on board, he'll start with the questions. Still, I take the helmet and jam it on. It's not like I want to spend the night in the parking lot (right now I feel the need for four walls and a door with a lock—and a fortress and a few cannons wouldn't come amiss either). Ubers are also in remarkably short supply in Big Bear too, so since I came with Pick, leaving with him just makes sense.

"You still don't want to know?" I concentrate on getting myself onto Pick's bike without landing on my butt. What is it with guys and difficult-to-board rides? Is it dick advertising? The bigger the wheels and the greater the distance from the ground to the seat, the bigger the penis?

Pick scrubs a hand over his head. Okay. He's not quite the Zen-like pool of tranquility he seems. "Not a question of my not wanting to know. When you're ready to tell, you'll share. If not, then no worries. I know how to wait. He's a nasty son-of-a-bitch, though. I'd feel better if I knew whatever you could tell me."

Such a pretty speech. I successfully lever my way onto the seat behind Pick. Wait for it… he reaches between us and pulls my arms round his waist. Then he turns his head and gives me another look. He seems to have an endless supply—and he's definitely waiting for an answer.

"He is. Nasty." I fight the urge to rub my arms. When I'm around Thad now, I feel like the gross slick just flies off him and sticks to me. In comparison, Pick's warm, solid, and safe.

Sometimes safe.

Right now, heat and danger practically radiate off the man.

"Figured." Pick does a quick visual check to make sure I'm secure, then backs us out of the parking spot. He drives with the same easy confidence he does everything, and if I want to plant myself in his lap and pretend we're riding off into the sunset on happy, happy horseback, that's either temporary weakness on my part or the fact that riding a motorcycle feels like I've just shoved the world's best vibrating dildo between my legs.

"We dated," I blurt out.

"Doesn't look like you got a happily-ever-after out of that," he observes. He doesn't take his eyes off the road, but I get the sense that he's entirely focused on me. And somehow, he hears me just fine despite the roar of the bike's pipes.

"Yeah. You could say that." *Do NOT climb into his lap.* I try not to sound pathetic, but I'm unexpectedly hosting a pity party back here, and I think he knows it. He exhales roughly, which seems to be the manly version of the sad panda sigh, and his hands tighten on the handle bars. Hopefully, he's imagining throttling Thad and not me. Not that I actually think Pick would ever hurt me, but he's only human despite all those super hero qualities he possesses. And apparently my inner Damsel in Distress thinks we should lean against him, despite the awkward seat set up, and hold on real tight. *No,* I tell her. This needs to be his call. Odds are good he loses patience with me, because nothing about this relationship will be easy.

And since when do we have a relationship anyhow?

Since you paid him a little midnight visit, the Damsel points out, sounding quite pleased with herself.

And sure he's rescued me from celibacy and given me my first hands-free orgasm in what feels like forever, but that's not really a relationship. Like one that involves talking. And feelings.

You're talking now, Damsel points out.

And you're feeling shit.

Damn her for being right.

Pick apparently gets tired of waiting for me to finish my internal monologue because he busts in. "There more to it than that?"

"Probably." *Absolutely.* I can practically feel Damsel gloating. She thinks this night is going to go her way.

"He going to be trouble?"

"He'll be back."

"I like trouble just fine." The helmet can't hide the slow grin tugging at the corner of Pick's mouth. When he looks like that, my panties are in serious jeopardy. Damsel and my inner hussy both urge us to reach on over and reward the man for his help tonight. In fact, I should totally reciprocate, right? Give him a helping hand wherever he'd like it? A roadside blow job?

"No worries there, honey," he continues. His dark eyes never leave the road, but I know he's aware of me, of how my fingers pick nervously at his T-shirt because Damsel really is winning and how I can't stop the betraying gesture. "Now would be a good time to tell me what happened."

Of course he's right, but that doesn't make the confession any easier. Who really likes to air all their sins?

"Let's just say that Thad and I have a past," I suggest. Maybe we can go for the simple, not-as-embarrassing executive summary and skimp on the details.

Pick's not on board with that. "I'm going to need details. This isn't a game of connect-the-dots where you throw out a few hints and I fill in the lines. Tell me what kind of trouble you're in."

"You can't help."

Truth, right? I mean, unless I need someone to beat the shit out of Thad and possibly help me hide the body. I let myself enjoy that fantasy for a moment. I know violence doesn't really solve anything, and I actually don't condone murder under any circumstances, but it's been a long night and I'm feeling weak.

"Try me." Mr. Safety First actually takes his eyes off the road to look back at me. It's a short glance, but he packs a lot into it. "Give me a chance, Sarah Jo."

Chances are risky business. I knew riding with Pick was a bad idea. I hate the fear I feel about what Thad might do to me, but that feeling isn't anywhere near as bad as the uncertainty. Thad Hill has decided to make my life his own personal playground, popping in and out with devastating effect. He won't just leave me alone. Somehow, I have to defuse the threat he poses, but I'm fresh out of genius plans. I tried going to the authorities and that was an epic disaster. Running was my Hail Mary pass and it failed, and I don't have much experience with standing my ground.

Pick, on the other hand, knows everything about holding his line. He's an expert on digging and refusing to be pushed back. One inch at a time, he takes back whatever ground fire has claimed, day in and day out, summer after summer.

"Four months ago." Start at the beginning, right? "I was living in Auburn, working as an in-home caregiver. There was a fire in my client's home."

Thank God, Mrs. Joan hadn't been home. No, she'd gone off on the bus to Bunco night like she always did on Thursday evenings. At least Thad had waited until the elderly woman was clear. I wasn't supposed to be there, either, but I'd forgotten my favorite sweater and swung back to get it just in time to catch the rat-thieving bastard pulling away from the curb. In hindsight, I realized that he'd popped the batteries in the smoke detectors during that visit, cracked a gas main, and set the microwave to go off. I'd got in, got out, too excited about my evening to notice the whiff of gas.

Stupid.

The timer went *ding* and Mrs. Joan's home blew up, taking most of her possessions with it. All fingers, of course, had pointed my way from the get-go. I was the last one in the house, and no one listened when I insisted that Thad's car had pulled away as I arrived. He was a deputy sheriff, just out and about doing his job. I got painted as the disgruntled girlfriend, because he immediately claimed we'd been having relationship problems, saying I'd wanted a ring and commitment, but he'd been unsure.

"The fire was suspicious?" Pick asks, proving he can connect the dots just fine without my help.

"I worked there, as a caregiver, and I was the last person in the house before the fire started."

"Was the owner okay?"

"Yeah. She'd gone to play Bunco over at the senior

center. She always did, like clockwork, every Thursday evening."

"Fires happen. What made this one your problem?"

This would be so much better if he didn't insist on details. Talking is highly overrated. "Because some diamond jewelry was missing, and the police report suggested someone had turned on the gas and then used the microwave to blow the place sky high."

I'm just grateful that the house was somewhat isolated from its neighbors. In a more crowded subdivision, there could have been collateral damage.

"I told the police about how I saw Thad that night," I admit "I ran back for a sweater I'd forgotten, and I saw him pulling away from the curb."

Pick doesn't interrupt me. And he's really listening, I realize. He hasn't dismissed my explanation. Yet. That focus is damned sexy, too. He's not handsome in a polished GQ kind of way. Instead, he's all rough, hard angles, from the strong line of his jaw to the small scars and burn marks scattered over his forearms and throat. He's not afraid to put his body on the line and that's better than a suit and a billion dollars any day. He doesn't even need a cape to be a hero, although my inner hussy promptly suggests that we should buy him one. He could wear it naked. I promise fun things would ensue. Personally, I think my inner hussy just doesn't want to finish this conversation.

"Coincidences happen," he suggests, sounding reluctant. That's Pick, though. He's fair and balanced. "Hell, I don't like the man, Sarah Jo. He's a bully and he's clearly jonesing for some revenge, but that doesn't make him an arsonist. You got some proof that we can use?"

"It doesn't. I confronted him."

Pick swears.

"And he threatened me," I continue. "No matter what I thought I knew, he said, no one would believe me. After all, he's the local deputy and I'm a recent arrival. One year doesn't count for much when most everyone has known Thad since he was a baby. I'm just the newbie on the block, fresh from San Francisco with my degree in hand and willing to do anything to earn a living because I have bills to pay and college wasn't cheap."

"When he comes back," Pick says, and I can't help but note his use of *when*, "that will make holding him off harder, if it's his word against yours. Have you considered lawyering up?"

"That takes money." Pick opens his mouth and wisely closes it when I shake my head. I'm so not taking his money. "I'll cross that bridge when I come to it."

He snorts. "Honey, you're already standing midstream. A bridge might be a blessing."

"I'll handle this."

He doesn't hesitate.

"You know that if you need help, all you got to do is ask."

"Thanks," I say way too awkwardly. This is my business, not his, but this are-we-in-a-relationship thing (*yes* Damsel in Distress and Inner Hussy scream in tandem) complicates everything.

"Uh-huh." He shakes his head, and the bike begins the familiar ascent to Baby Bear Lodge. "Well, you change your mind, you know where to find me, okay? There's no expiration date on that offer."

SARAH JO

I HEAR PICK humming before I see him. Okay, so I actually ogle his feet and not the entire man, but details. I can say with great authority that *The Voice* will not be beating down his door anytime soon—he may be super hot in the looks department, but he's spectacularly untalented in all things musical. If I'm not mistaken, he's performing an off-key version of "99 Bottles of Beer." The fire camp boasts a block of plumbed showers, which puts the place in luxury territory as far as the hotshots go. Personally, I'm much more particular. Running water—particularly *hot* water—isn't optional in my book. Which is yet another reason I'm clearly a city kind of girl and entirely fish out of water here. The showers are very utilitarian, all get-in and get-out, which makes it easy to spot Pick. In case I need more clues, he's tossed his towel over the shower rod and left his clothes neatly folded on a nearby lawn chair.

All evidence points to Pick being naked, so I take a brief moment to enjoy the mental image and some favorite memories. He has a spectacular body, undoubtedly from all that firefighting he does. When you drag heavy equipment all over a mountain, you develop yummy muscles. I guess it's Karma's way of making up for the whole daily risking-of-lives thing. I may also imagine grabbing that neat stack and running. He'll laugh. And then he'll get even. It might even include naked pursuit through the camp because I'm fast discovering that Pick doesn't care what other people think. I don't mean that in a selfish way, either. It's just that he has strong ideas of right and wrong, and doesn't deviate from them because of a little crowd-sourcing or negative public opinion. And honestly? I wouldn't mind if Pick pursued me.

Yay cheers Inner Hussy.

This gives me an idea, and I'm out of my shorts and tank top in under two minutes. A quick shimmy takes care of my panties as well. The summer heat makes a bra pure torture, so I skipped it. It's thunderstorm weather, or so I've been warned, and each breath I take is sticky and heavy. There'll be lightning later, white bolts that slice down from the sky and strike the trees. The entire camp will be searching for smokes where the lightning's strike has smoldered long enough to flare up into flames.

I'm working on some lightning of my own.

Pulling back the shower curtain far enough to slip through, I step into the shower. Pick is soaping up, back to the door, and for just a minute I stand there and admire my view. Soap and water slick the powerful muscles of his shoulders as he ducks his head beneath the spray.

Showtime.

"You got room for one more?"

I barely get the words out, before he turns in a smooth, powerful move that leaves me up against the wall, his arm over my throat. Pick would never hurt me, but this rougher side of him is kind of (really super) sexy. He can and will take care of himself in a fight or a tight spot, and I like that. Unfortunately, I seem to like everything about him.

He blinks down at me, looking a little dazed. I guess he's not so good with surprises. I make a mental note to cross the surprise birthday party off my list. There might be accidental casualties.

"Hell." He doesn't sound upset, just taken aback.

"Surprise?" I offer. Thanks to his ninja warrior move, my breasts are squashed against his chest. When I exhale, my nipples rub against the rough dusting of hair on his forearms. This little accident feels so good that I do it again on purpose. His eyes darken, which I take as a sign of approval.

"Did I miss the memo about water conservation?" A smile tugs at his lips.

"Conservation is very important," I agree, tilting my head back to see his face better. When I draw a leg up his, part of him makes it clear that surprise shower intrusions aren't all bad, because he's now sporting one very impressive erection. He's hot and slick, so I just have to angle myself against him for an even better fit. We're kind of perfect together.

"Yeah." He whips his arm away from my throat, as if he's only just realized he's on me like a caveman, but he doesn't move away. Instead, he leans in closer, planting his arms on either side of my head. "You in the mood for a shower or something?"

"Can I vote for or something?"

When he smiles, he gets this little crinkle around the edges of his eyes. Probably from the sun—or from laughter. I like that about him. He enjoys life. The same way he enjoys my body. Wholeheartedly, rolling with whatever punches life tosses him. Too bad I can't be more like that. I've just never been a particularly laid back kind of person—I'm more of a worry wart, although it seems like Pick can work with that.

"You planning on starting something right here in the shower?"

Sometimes the doing is even better than the planning. I press my mouth against the firm line of his jaw, loving the rasp of his ten-o'clock shadow against my lips. That has to be why I'm practically humming with pleasure (and not "99 Bottles of Beer"). It has to explain why I shamelessly run my fingers over his skin wherever I can reach. There's just so much Pick to love that I'm not sure where to start.

"I won't start anything I can't finish," I promise, tracing my lips over his throat and down his chest. He tastes like soap and man, which are now officially my favorite flavors. He's feeling cooperative too because he holds still for me, letting me touch him however I want. So I do because this man totally deserves a reward. I lick away the water from the shower, swirling my tongue over his stiff nipples before I head lower. My body tightens with anticipation because this is going to be good.

"Sarah Jo—" He tugs on my hair, a little rougher than is strictly necessary because the man already has my full attention.

"Uh-uh." I reach up and circle his nipple with my finger before pinching lightly. It's not much as far as kinky sex acts go because the sad truth is, I'm a pretty vanilla person. He doesn't seem to mind, though. He groans, his fingers flexing in my hair. My clit gives a little pulse in time to the sound. I don't know why working him up gets me going too, but it does. I want to do him in the shower even though there's an entire camp outside and someone's going to know.

His stomach definitely qualifies as a work of art. It's all hard ridges and sexy muscle. Usually I'd be busy comparing his and hers—and I definitely sport more of a beer keg than a six-pack myself—but right now I'm just letting myself enjoy. Who wouldn't like having a big, sexy, *hung* hotshot at her mercy? So I take full advantage, running my hands down all those gorgeous muscles and nipping lightly, although it's harder than you'd think because there's not an inch of give in his abdomen.

And speaking of inches… there's a whole lot of inches going on down below. The man's practically packing a yardstick, and I've got a ringside seat. His dick is huge, and I have some dirty, dirty plans for it. I wrap a hand around the hard length, and miracle of miracles, my fingers can't meet. He's such a keeper. His groan gets a little deeper, a little rougher. Somebody's feeling impatient. I pull my hand away for a second, lick the palm, and wrap my present back up. I'd go for the soap, but that would make stage two in this plan less fun for me.

I work his dick, sliding my palm up and down. At some point, I add my other hand because it wants in on the action, too. And there's something about choosing to go down on my knees, about just taking my time and getting lost in the moment, a decadent rhythm that's in no rush and yet headed only one place. Eventually he tugs on my hair again, trying to pull me up. I think he might be worried he'll come on my face, which is sweet but I'm nowhere near done with him.

"This is my turn." I look up at him. "You're just going to have to stand there and take it, big guy."

His laughter rumbles over my head as his hands stop their tugging. He braces himself against the wall, palms flat against the tile. "Now there's a hard thing."

The muscles of his abdomen demand more attention. The shiny scar from a burn is impossible to miss, a visible reminder of the risks he takes each day of the summer. I'll just have to kiss what I can better.

"You didn't win that fight." I press my mouth against the mark while my hands keep using his dick as my own personal slip-and-slide. I kiss over his ribs and down his stomach. Kiss lower, brushing my cheek against the tip of his dick.

"Can't win them all." The words come out hoarse and needy. "Sarah Jo—"

"Shhhh." I rub my cheek against him again. He's all hard wrapped up in velvety goodness. "I'm not done here."

He can't say I didn't warn him, right? I suck him into my mouth, wrapping my lips around the thick, slick head. His hips shift hard when I start sucking. His head hits the side of the shower, and his fingers find my hair again. I kiss and suck, swirling my tongue around his enormous cock like I'm inking his skin with our own design. He wraps me up, pulling me closer with his arms and legs, covering me with his big body. It's almost overwhelming, but this is Pick. I need him close.

I need all of him.

I take as much of him in my mouth as I can, wrapping a hand around the inches I can't cover. There's a whole lot of Pick, and it's hard to choose my favorite spot. So I explore. I run my tongue up the bulging vein, pressing against the spot beneath the head. The hands in my hair tense.

Definitely mine right now.

"Sarah Jo," he bites out.

I pop off just long enough to answer him. "Yeah, baby?"

It takes him a few minutes to answer the question because I part my lips and go right back to sucking him. I work him with my tongue, moving from the tip to the base and then back up again. He's so hard and getting harder with each stroke. He's exactly what I need to hold onto, someone solid in the shit storm that is my life. *And maybe not just in the stormy parts*, something whispers in my head. I don't think that's my inner Damsel in Distress, either. It might be my heart, but I'm not listening.

Pick groans something that sounds like a curse. "Tell me you're stopping, because I'm not."

Nope. No intention of stopping here.

And then he totally loses control. He pushes through the tight ring of my lips before popping back out again. I take him as deep as I can, not wanting this to end.

I need this.

I need him.

PICK

I FUCK her mouth. Not sure what else to call it, but the sight of my dick sliding in and out of Sarah Jo's pretty pink mouth makes me feel dirty as sin and twice as blissful as heaven. Sarah Jo on her knees, wrapped around me like I'm her favorite flavor of sweet, is the most erotic sight I've ever seen. Her water-slicked hair makes her look like a naughty mermaid, naked, kneeling. Needing.

She moans, and the sound starts in my dick and plays straight up to my heart. She doesn't seem to mind that I'm driving faster and harder, hammering in and out of her mouth like it's her pussy. It feels so goddamned good. Better than anything anyone's ever done for me before, which is why I'm seconds away from blowing down her throat and then yanking out and painting her tits with my jizz. Watching her take me isn't helping me hold back any, either. We need to slow this down before I disgust her.

"Christ, Sarah Jo. You want to pull back? I'm not going to last."

Her eyes twinkle up at me, and fuck me, but she doesn't let go. Not one inch.

Instead, she sucks me back in deep, her tongue rubbing my dick until I can't take it, and I blow up harder than a goddamned forest fire. There's a fucking inferno in my balls, and Sarah Jo is the only cure. I come, hard and fast, and she swallows me down. She's not letting go, not now, and my whole world is nothing and no one but Sarah Jo, right there on her knees, giving me something I hadn't known I needed.

"Fuck me," I grit out. Those aren't the poetic words she deserves. They're not the pretty words that would tell her how much I enjoyed what she just did. But I've got nothing. She smiles and swallows, and I shudder and curse and try to pretend that she hasn't completely undone me. She reaches around me and flips off the water, which is already running lukewarm. The next Rogue into the shower is gonna curse me.

Or cheer.

There should definitely be cheering.

With a small smile, Sarah Jo pulls my towel off the rod, wipes her mouth, and hands it to me. Holy. FUCK.

And then she says the only thing that could make today better. Well, other than maybe three little words that I've previously thought belonged on a candy heart, but that I'm starting to want to hear from her.

"You want to go make that RV of yours rock?"

"Hell, yeah." I drag on my shorts, wrap the towel around her, and pull her up into my arms. "You've got a turn coming to you, honey."

SARAH JO

AFTER TOO many hours on my feet, I'm glad to curl up for my dinner break and hold a book instead of a spatula. The way I see it, I have forty-five perfect alone-time minutes until I have to return to the cafeteria, and I plan to maximize each and every one of them. Because fire camp tends toward the primitive and there's not a whole lot of places to go to get away from everyone on your break unless you're partial to trees and bushes, the cooks have rigged up an impromptu break room in the small building that doubles as a pantry. In addition to a stunning quantity of industrial-grade metal shelving holding a lifetime supply of tomato sauce and syrup, there are two bright green plastic lawn chairs, plenty of pillows, a small TV, and whatever else the girls have left behind over years of stolen breaks. We've nicknamed our hidey hole the Chateau du Nap, and while I suspect it's not quite so secret, it's still pretty sweet.

Since I'm the only one on break right now, no one will bother me, and I've got my butt planted on a chair and a mountain of pillows at my back. I've also got a drink, a snack, and the book. Right now, however, the story in my hands isn't working its usual magic. Instead of losing myself in the world of Highlanders, I'm thinking about making a field trip to camp and finding Pick's RV.

Again.

For the third time this week.

We'd made a mad dash to his RV after I heated him up in the shower. He'd shoved open the door and all but scooped me up in his arms, his hands on my butt as he'd carried me over to his big bed. Then, he'd proceeded to reclaim his towel, kissing every inch he'd uncovered. I'm pretty sure half the camp heard me shrieking his name, but no one said anything. Even Rosalie hadn't done much more than smile and high-five me. She's still convinced that fire camp is a synonym for *matchmaking service*.

But cozying up here alone is, well, *alone*. I have a serious Pick addiction, and hooking up with him isn't curing me. If anything, I'm getting worse. Now I want to spend the entire night wrapped up in his arms, whether we're banging like crazed bunnies or sleeping. Or talking. So far, the only F-word we've exchanged has been *fuck*, but I'm sensing that *feelings* aren't far behind. I'm not sure what to do.

I turn the page. Nope. The Highlander in my book isn't doing it for me tonight, no matter how hot he is in his kilt. I'm apparently Team Pick, and right now I can't think of a single good reason why I shouldn't head on over in his direction after I finish work and make myself at home with his big body.

I'm still thinking that through (and coming up empty on the reasons to-not-to) when the lights flicker and then go out. Crap. Closing the book, I set it gently on the bed. Even Mother Nature and the local electric company think I should Pick over print, so who am I to argue?

Sliding off the lawn chair, I feel my way over to the window. Power outages aren't uncommon, and the average age of a building in the fire camp is downright geriatric. When I look out, though, the rest of the buildings still shine with light. I jiggle the light switch by the door, but no dice. Maybe I've blown a fuse.

The door opens behind me, and I turn with a smile. We cooks stick together. Rosalie has likely sent a rescue party. Or an electrician. Either one works for me since I'm standing in the dark. There's just enough light from the window to let me see the shadow of a man stepping inside. It's probably Hunter, Lola's main squeeze. He's handy and extremely useful to have around, so I'm not above borrowing him to handle my electrical emergency.

"Fuse box?" I ask.

"That's one way of looking at it." Thad's voice is an unfortunate cold dose of reality. He shuts the door carefully behind him, and I hear the snick of the lock as he flips the deadbolt.

"You got a warrant this time?" My voice doesn't shake. That makes me proud, because I have a feeling my knees are shaking visibly. Being locked up anywhere with Thad is a recipe for disaster. I don't need the light to know there's a whole lot of ugly written on his face. For a long moment, he doesn't move, doesn't speak. The bastard's spinning out the sickening anticipation and it's working.

"That's a real nice getup." He gestures toward my shorts and tank top with his service weapon. Which is *drawn.* I rub suddenly clammy palms on said shorts. He's between me and the door. The window isn't much of a possibility, either, too small for a quick exit. I'd never kick out the screen before he was on me. He stares, thinking God knows what (but the gun's a bad sign as is the lack of a warrant) and I panic. The soft *whup-whup* of the slowing overhead fan is the only thing filling in the silence.

Think. I need a plan.

My inner Damsel in Distress is praying for a miracle and a white knight, my inner hussy is all no freaking way, and my bad ass side seems to have gone on vacation or perhaps she's run for help. All I can do is stall for more time because I don't think I really want to find out why he's here. "What do you want, Thad?"

He flashes me his crooked smile. Once upon a time, I thought that smile charming, which just goes to show that appearances are deceiving. His answer does nothing to reassure me, either.

"We've gone over this before. You need to come back with me."

"So you do have a warrant?" I'm betting that's a no. And it's interesting, too, because if he could, he'd get one just to rub my face in it.

"Not yet," he spat. "But I will. And it doesn't matter anyhow. You're going back with me, Sarah Jo."

His thumb, stroking the barrel of his gun, makes a compelling case. Warrant or no warrant, he holds all the cards right now, and my options are decidedly limited. Problem is, the fire camp isn't exactly teeming with life right now. The hotshots are all out in the field, eating dinner, or in town getting their fun on. And even if I scream, how do I know any big, burly guys in the vicinity correctly interpret my desperate screech as *call 911 and send an army of vengeful giants armed for bear* as opposed to *ooh itsy bitsy spider sighting?* (they've stopped running to the rescue after a few false alarms). I'm on my own here, and while that's usually how I prefer my life, I'd like to make an exception tonight.

"You've got to pay the piper, Sarah Jo," he says as if we're discussing a five-dollar bet or a dare and not my life. Because I suspect he's all in. He wants me to pay, and he's not going to shortchange his revenge.

I take a shot at the truth. "I did nothing wrong."

"You shouldn't have run and tattled," he accuses. "You said things."

"Nobody believed me." This is, most unfortunately, also the truth.

"Maybe. Maybe not. Eventually, someone might. You should have been on my side."

There's zero reason for me to side with him, but I don't thinking pointing that out would be prudent. Instead, I go for wishful thinking. "I'm not going anywhere with you."

In answer, he unhooks a pair of handcuffs from his utility belt. "You're not the one in charge here. I am. Turn around and face the wall. Put your hands behind you."

I let Pick do things to me last night. Sensual, playful, demanding things. He turned me inside out and reduced me to a quivering, compliant puddle. I still haven't quite figured out how I feel about that, but I know this is wrong. Giving up control to Thad isn't some kind of dirty game, and I don't trust him.

Not like I trust Pick.

I take a deep breath (because if it's my last one, I want to make it a good one) and flip him off.

"What the hell is wrong with you? You want me to shoot you?"

Absolutely not. I back the hell up, but he's already coming for me. At least he shoves the gun back into its holster, so he's either given up on shooting me or he's decided to do it by hand. And then he lunges, fists shooting toward my face, and I retreat as fast and as far as I can. Of course, it's not enough. His fist clips my jaw, sending me crashing to the floor. Pain blazes across my cheek, but I'm not dead and this is no time to stop. I scramble up.

He shakes his head, hooks his leg around mine, and yanks. I promptly end up back on the floor.

"Gotcha." I can hear the smile in his voice as he pins me down with his weight. If I can just get him off, I can make the door . . . I buck, trying to knock him off balance, but he rolls me easily, jamming a knee into the small of my back. Then he pulls back hard on my arms, and my back bows helplessly.

"Stop fighting," he demands, "and you'll be happier."

Is he freaking crazy? I mean, the answer,

obviously, is yes, but what makes him think I'll just give in now and let him do whatever it is that he's planning? Because I don't think he's about to give me a free vacation to some lovely tropical destination with unlimited margaritas.

"Bite me." He's bigger and better trained, and apparently that whole thing about people performing superhuman feats because of adrenaline-fueled desperation? That's not happening here. I end up stuck on the floor, panting as I gaze longingly at the enormous tin cans of tomatoes so tantalizingly close. I totally bet I could bash Thad's head in with one of those if he would just hold still.

"There's a good girl." Thad's satisfied voice fills my ear. God. It's so gross. His erection presses into my lower back. I buck again, but he's still bigger and stronger. My shoulders burn as he jerks my arms toward him.

The zip-ties tighten around my wrists.

PICK

I NEED TO FIND Sarah Jo. I don't know if it's because I'm desperate to see her, or because I miss her, or just because somehow she's a part of my life now—a part that matters a whole lot. I'm not a relationship Einstein, but even I know that we've got something going on. We may not be labeling shit, but we're still feeling it.

Okay. I'm feeling it. Who the hell knows what's going on in Sarah Jo's head? I spend most of the drive back to fire camp trying to figure it out, but give it up when I run out of road and hit the parking lot. I could drive to Timbuktu and still not find the answers I'm looking for. So I'll just have to ask.

Words.

Words suck.

I should have swung by the Hallmark store instead of the florist. Tonight could be my lucky night, though. Perhaps when she gets off work, Sarah Jo will be in the mood to play show instead of tell, and she'll get my message. I glance across at the passenger side seat. So I brought flowers. A dozen red roses because the Internet claims nothing says *I love you* like red roses. Or a big fucking diamond, but I'm trying to do the woo—not scare my girl off. And while I'm not a flowers kind of guy, I'd like to think I can change for Sarah Jo. Or if I can't change, I can at least polish up the rough edges a little.

She deserves white picket fences and happily-ever-after. Part of me wants to give her the big-ass diamond and a five-bedroom McMansion in the suburbs. The other, wiser part of me knows I can't. Sure I've got more than enough money to live, but no one gets rich working fire crews, and I've always been a simple man with simple tastes. Fire camp has been enough for me.

Until now.

I pull in as quietly as I can because I don't really want an audience for my flower-toting self. I'd never live it down, and if I crash and burn, I'm gonna need some alone time to lick my wounds. The place seems pretty much deserted, however. There's a handful of familiar trucks, a couple of beat-up sedans that belong to the cooks, and Sarah Jo's POS car. The damn grin is back on my face. Just the thought of seeing her, even at the other end of a plate of food, makes me smile.

That's when I realize that there's a patrol car tucked in the darkest corner of the makeshift parking lot. *Fuck.* I don't need spidey senses to know that something's wrong. Sarah Jo attracts trouble like nobody's business, and Thad Hill made his intentions perfectly clear. I'm betting that car belongs to Deputy Douche.

SARAH JO

THAD drags me to my feet, pulling his gun from its holster and pressing the barrel against my side. "We're walking out of here."

I'd like to say *Like hell*, but he's won this round. The pain in my face fades some, leaving me clearheaded. He can't keep me here, not for what he intends. He wants the glory of bringing me in. The pleasure of punishing me for defying him. None of that counts for shit if he can't get me out the door and into his car. I guess preventing that is my new, best plan.

He gives me a small shake. "You got that?"

"Yeah." I really, really do.

"Then shut up and start walking." He wraps an arm around me, dragging me up against his side. The feel of his body touching mine makes me want to gag. I've touched him before, although never the way I've touched

Pick, but this is wrong on so many levels. Ironically, though, Thad and I actually want the same thing at this moment. My only chance lies outside, in the four hundred yards of opportunity on the way to his car.

Plus, would he really shoot me? Right outside where everyone can see? He plans on forcing me to go with him, but that requires a degree of cooperation from me, and he's definitely counting on me being scared.

And on the handcuffs.

When I flex my wrists, the plastic digs into my skin. There's zero give, so whatever I do next, I do it bound and trussed. I decide it's probably best if I don't worry overmuch about that. One step at a time, right?

Thad flips the lock, opens the door, and steps out like *he's* got no worries. With the electricity out, the light over the door is out, too, leaving us in the shadows. Plus, most folks are now focused on getting the lights back on—and so they're not going to worry when a cook doesn't show up promptly after her break. I could be asleep, trapped in the loo, or any one of a dozen other things.

The gun digs into my rib cage, a not-so-subtle reminder that right now he's very much the one in charge. Have I mentioned how much I hate losing control? It's not like this is a revelation, but my current lack of choices just reinforces what I've known all along. Men suck, being powerless sucks, and sometimes life serves up an enormous bowl of suck and all you can do is wait for a chance to trade up to something better. Which also sucks.

"Nice and easy," Thad cautions, as if sticking his gun in my ribs hasn't already made his point. I think he's just rubbing it in at this point, which fits with what I know about him. He guides me down the porch, all faux solicitousness, and along the edge of the camp, sticking to the shadows and the trees. Well, I didn't expect him to march me straight down the middle, right? I'll just have to watch a little more closely for my opportunity.

He monologues like a bad villain, too. It's all *you're going to be sorry blah fucking blah I've got you now.* I get it, and yes, I'm sorry. Sorry I ever fell for his charm. Sorry I didn't do things differently with Mrs. Joan. Sorry I didn't take a chance on Pick and me. There's this weird ache in my chest that I can't even rub because I'm trussed up like a Thanksgiving turkey. It's not a heart attack, though, or even heartburn. It takes me half the distance to the parking lot to realize the sad truth. It's heartache, and how stupid is that to only figure out now that I want *things* with Pick? Things like feelings and emotions and maybe possibly spending a whole lot of time with him? I'm not sure how that would work since we both like to be in charge, but now it looks like I'll never know. I add that to my list of things that suck.

In a moment, I'm sure I'll come up with an awesome, super successful plan to get away from Thad, march my butt to the nearest police station and try—again—to get someone to listen to me. The only way to fix that, though, is to deal with Thad, and that means somehow getting away from him. Or I can sell a kidney and lawyer up. Or… I could ask Pick for help. He has ideas. He *wants* to help. And I think I might be okay with letting him, as long as I can choose the plan and can return the favor some day. I don't have to make him the boss of me—just take turns standing watch with him. And that seems like another relationship thing, me guarding his back and him guarding mine. It's like the emotional equivalent of soaping each other's back in the shower. Some spots are hard to reach or feel better when someone else gets them.

Halfway to the parking lot, I lunge. It's not my best idea, because he immediately gets an arm around my throat. Two hundred yards has done nothing to change the weight/height ratio between us any—he's still taller and stronger. Pulling my head into his shoulder, he squeezes until breathing becomes my primary focus. *God.* In and out, little shallow pants, until he eases up because he's made his point, and no, apparently he doesn't want to kill me in the fire camp.

"Don't," he snarls. "Be smart about this."

There's no answer for that kind of demand, and it doesn't matter. The boom that shakes the ground around us swallows up anything I might have said. The camp lights up like the Fourth of July, flames shooting into the sky from the direction where we're headed.

"Flammables shed," Thad observes. He's practically cackling, he's so gleeful. "They really should have had someone watching that."

He's crazy. This is a fire camp full of firefighters—not a military compound. The shed was pointed out to me when I first came up here to cook—it's a definite no smoking zone—and it's where the hotshots lock up their fusees and flamethrowers. It also houses a small arsenal of drip torches, gas cans, and a dozen different kinds of oil.

"That's my insurance, right there," Thad continues,

towing me along faster. Behind us, shouts and curses ring out as the hotshots spring into action, everyone running toward the flames and away from Thad and me.

I definitely need help. I'm not getting out of this on my own. Just to prove the point, the parking lot looms up before us and I spot Thad's patrol car. Once he gets me in that backseat, it's game over. He'll drive; I'll lose. I'll be nothing more than a footnote in the morning paper.

Scream for help.

Thoughts flash through my head, lightning-bug fast, but none of them prevent the patrol car from getting closer. I don't want to do it. I don't *like* doing it. Asking for help—and trusting someone else to provide it—isn't how I live. Of course, changing up how I do things—since right now all that's managed to do is to get me dragged forcibly across a fire camp—is just smart. I realize Pick did a whole lot of offering, while I did my best to push him away except when we were having sex. Then I stuck close, but I'm not sure that counts. He could have given up on me, but he hasn't. He stuck up for me when Thad made his previous appearances. So it shouldn't be so hard to ask for his help now, to be smart about this.

I hate doing the smart thing.

The *good* thing, though, is that Thad Hill clearly thinks he has me all figured out—and that I'll go quietly into that good night (or really freaking awful nightmare—you guess which one it's going to be). Dragging my heels, maybe, but he doesn't expect me to want to draw attention to myself or to pull in anyone else. Not really. If he had, he'd have knocked me unconscious or figured out a different exit strategy.

Pick's been on me to change, so here goes nothing. I open my mouth and bellow.

"Pick Revere, get your ass over here now."

Simple. Clear. Always in control. That's me.

Okay, so I'm not totally in control of this Thad thing (at all), but I'm bringing Pick in on my terms.

"Fu—" Thad slams a hand over my mouth and picks up the pace… and cue step two in my impromptu break-free-and-live-happily-ever-after plan. I dig my heels into the gravel, go limp as a pissed-off toddler—and bite his hand. Hard.

He tastes every bit as bad as I feared.

PICK

SARAH JO hollers my name like a drill sergeant barking orders. I've learned a few critical lessons during our fuckfests. First, while naked is fun with Sarah Jo and I love making her come, our time spent out of bed is pretty amazing, too. She's slowly letting me in, and I've been careful not to spook her. She'll let me finger her clit, shove my face into her pussy and eat her until she screams, but opening up her head or letting me in on what she's thinking doesn't happen as fast. So I've made getting to know her my new mission.

One of the things I've learned? Sarah Jo doesn't like asking for—or accepting—help. She's a DIY queen when it comes to her life, so her urgent summons is out of character. She's working tonight and it's the right time for her to be on her break, but the girls' impromptu breakroom is empty and dark, the lights out of order. I'm still recovering from my mad sprint over there when a summer's worth of fusees explode and suddenly we've got fire in our own backyard.

Exploding fusees.

Unexpected patrol car.

You see where I'm headed with this?

Why I need to see for myself that she's safe?

After I hold and squeeze her and probably say plenty of stupid shit, she can retreat back to Emotionarctica and I'll try to respect those boundaries. So I reverse my mad dash and head toward her voice. It's never a good sign when Sarah Jo asks for help. I think. Because it's *never fucking happened before*, and I don't want to think it's in any way connected to the sheriff's cruiser and the explosion.

I tear toward the parking lot, fielding strange looks and what-the-fucks from the guys on my team. Who are all running the *other* way, toward the fire that needs putting out ASAP. Something smaller goes up, lending another snap, crackle, and boom to the night and drowning out Sarah Jo's follow-up demand.

Three hundred yards. Two. *There*.

Thad Hill has definitely paid a return visit, the son-of-a-bitch. I should have followed up and made sure that Hill's superiors knew exactly what their deputy was up to, but I didn't. Sarah Jo clearly hadn't wanted the attention that kind of complaint would get, and I'd gone along with her wishes. I won't make that mistake again. Safety first, feelings second.

Thad wrestles with Sarah Jo, trying to open his car

door and keep her under control. She's putting up one hell of a fight, making Thad's job as difficult as possible. It's probably weird that I want to be the only one she gives a hard time. The only one who's special. The worry and anger erases that strange feeling.

Fortunately, I have a ready-made target for my aggression. I launch myself at Thad, fists flying. He doesn't see me coming, which is also satisfying. Sarah Jo has him distracted, which just goes to show that she and I make a good team. If I'm lucky, I'll be able to convince her to pick my side permanently when all this is over. My fist connects with Thad's jaw, snapping his head back with a satisfying crack.

Unfortunately, I don't knock his head off his neck. He drops Sarah Jo—a plus, because she promptly scrambles out of reach. The downside is that this frees up Thad's hands to pull his gun. Guns always make things messy.

We've got five feet between us, and Thad has the gun's business end pointing straight at my stomach. He's too close to miss, and I like my insides exactly as God made them. I don't need Thad redecorating or rearranging. He might not pull the trigger, but I can't take the chance. If I go down, Thad will just go after

Sarah Jo again. When she inches away from us, Thad pans the gun between us, so encouraging her to run away isn't going to work, either.

"Let's talk," I suggest. Not that I think using my words is going to resolve this particular situation, but it will buy me some time to come up with a better plan.

"I'm voting I get in the car and take Sarah Jo with me."

See? I don't like that plan.

"I can't let you do that." I decide it's probably best if I keep up my side of the conversation. Hopefully, Thad isn't the kind of guy who can shoot, talk, and cover my girl at the same time. Keeping my hands relaxed on my thighs, I assess the situation. Sarah Jo is still too close to Thad. The best option is for me to go in hard and fast. I'm pretty sure I can kill him before his bullets do for me, but I'd rather keep this as my backup plan because it definitely means I don't get a happily-ever-after with Sarah Jo.

"I don't see how you're stopping me." A mean smile cracks Hill's face. "Seeing as how I have the gun and you don't."

He doesn't get that if only one person walks away from this shit, it's Sarah Jo. Sure, I'd rather be walking with her, but that's not the only option I'm okay with. If I have to let her go and send her on ahead of me, she walks free. It's that simple.

I've never learned how to give up. It's been pointed out to me that a great many people would consider this to be a major character flaw. Fuck them. I've spent years fighting fires that are bigger, stronger, and more stubborn than me. And I've won. Even when I've had to temporarily step back and let the fire burn for a bit, the fire always, always goes out. Hill is simply a different kind of fire, and I'm going to shut him down, too.

I test the waters, easing my foot forward an inch. Hill shakes his head. "Uh-uh. Stay right where you are."

Gotcha. If I roll, it has to be a fast rush. On the other hand, that's definitely a Glock in Hill's hand. That means there's no safety standing between me and the first shot. If Hill has a full chamber, he'll have multiple opportunities to hurt someone.

"No worries," I say easily. Like we're having a fucking picnic or we just ran out of cold beer.

"Sarah Jo—" Thad doesn't take his eyes off me, which is too bad. "You get your ass in that car now. We're out of here. You move again, hotshot, and I'll drop you."

The nickname is endearing, but I need to wrap this up and get my girl out of here. I need her safe.

"Nope," she blurts out.

Seriously? I add paddling her cute ass to my to do list. When a deranged maniac is holding you at gunpoint, you give him the words he wants. And *then* you go with your boyfriend's secret escape plan. She and I need to get on the same page ASAP. Plus, I want her inside the car. Those patrol cars have bulletproof glass, and, even if the door stays open, she'll have more cover there.

Thad can't cover both of us if she moves as he's ordered. I think Sarah Jo must have figured that out for herself, because she springs into action. Jesus. Fucking. Christ. I'm supposed to be the one rescuing her, but she sweeps her leg out in a solid roundhouse and nails Thad in the back of his knees. Thad staggers, gun waving wildly, but he doesn't go down. Good. She's left something for me to do here. I move, going in fast and hard.

"Bitch." Thad screams the word like it's a bad thing, and points the gun in Sarah Jo's direction. Or tries to. I bitchslap that sucker, slamming my palm into the barrel and pushing up. That puts Thad's first shot up into the trees.

I hug Thad's arm tight, throwing all my weight into it as I bring my knee up and my head forward like I'm speeding down the fucking highway in all kinds of rush. My head smashes into Hill's forehead at the same moment I drive my knee into his groin. What happens next is a whole lot of screaming as I put the other man on the ground, twisting his wrist and taking possession of the gun.

"Told you, you wanted to be talking." I remove the chamber and pocket it, tossing the gun behind me.

Emptying the gun is as much for Thad's protection as it is Sarah Jo's. I want to kill this fucker so badly. He hurt my girl. He terrorized her. I don't think he deserves do-overs, second chances, or even a nice, comfy jail cell and decades of alone time, do you? I might also be headed straight for caveman territory because I also want to pick Sarah Jo up, toss her over my shoulder, and hole up somewhere with her. She could have been hurt. Hurt more than she already has been. Tearing Thad apart with my utility knife or just stomping the ever living fuck out of him with my steel-toes both seem like fair options. Sarah Jo will probably want to weigh in on Thad's future, however, so I need to dial my caveman back.

When I look away from Thad, I find her fast enough. Of course she hasn't taken advantage of the opportunity to run, fall back, or make a strategic retreat. She looks pissed, so maybe she's over being scared. That's good. I do a quick visual inventory since my hands are busy mauling Thad, but she looks okay. No blood or visible puncture wounds, although she's definitely mussed up, and Thad has zip-tied her hands behind her back. Once I've handed Thad off, I'll strip her down and check every inch. Kiss her better too, if she'll let me.

"You okay?"

While she thinks over her answer, I flip Hill over and plant my knee in his back harder than is strictly necessary. And wouldn't you know it? A quick rummage through the man's utility belt reveals a lifetime supply of zip-ties. I suspect he likes tying people up more than he should. I'm all for kink, but I'm also a fan of consenting, adult partners. I secure his wrists with a pair, and then add a second for good measure.

"Sarah Jo?" I prompt. I still need a verbal on that question of mine.

"I'm fine," she says, twisting to look at her wrists.

"I'm holding you to that."

That's all I have time to say because the noise approaching us says that our backup has arrived. Four hotshots have peeled off from the group effort to extinguish our supply shed. They're big-ass, mean sons-of-bitches, which fits the bill nicely. Deputy Douche won't pass Go and won't collect two hundred dollars or my girl—he's headed straight for jail unless my boys kill him first.

"You need a hand? Or just help burying the body?" Colt's gaze flicks between Hill and Sarah Jo. As a former race car driver, he's used to making split-second decisions and I'm pretty sure he's figured out the situation here. He certainly doesn't question why I have an officer of the law pinned and cuffed.

I fucking love my team.

That's when I realize that I'm including Sarah Jo in that number. She and I, we make a good team. We have each other's backs, and I respect the fuck out of her. And yeah, I love her, too. It's not something I've tried before, loving my woman, but I'm eager to get started.

"I'm betting Hill here is responsible for our latest fire."

"You think?" Hunter moves in casually. The hard look in his eyes bodes badly for Hill. Hunter gets cranky as shit when you blow up his fire camp. "Let's play Twenty Questions."

A subtle flick of Hunter's wrist, and the rest of our team surrounds Hill.

Thad pants, clearly realizing that he's outnumbered. Still, he manages to sneer, and my knuckles itch to be reintroduced to his face.

"You can't do this," Thad whines.

"Looks like I can." Hunter steps in closer, conveniently blocking Sarah Jo's view. Did I mention that I love this guy?

"You stole from an old lady," I drawl. I'd make an awesome detective.

"Prove it." Thad stares up at me defiantly. He's gonna make this hard.

"Not sure I have to. When we all go back to Auburn and turn your sorry ass in for stalking and kidnapping, you don't think the good folks there are going to ask why you went after Sarah Jo? They're going to turn you inside out, Hill. Wherever you hid the shit you stole, they'll find it."

"Will not." Hill's eyes flicker. *Gotcha.*

"Let me give you a couple of tips about confessing," Hunter offers, leaning down. He gets his mouth real near Hill's ear and whispers something that makes the other man turn pale.

"You can't do that."

"Try me." Hunter shrugs and then he smiles. A slow, cold smile that's one hundred percent mean. I'm glad I'm not the one on my knees.

"That old lady didn't need that stuff," Hill protests like the dumbass he is. He tries to struggle up, but surrounded as he is by hotshots, he goes straight back down again.

"You did this just for the money?" Sarah Jo's voice shakes, and then she gets it under control. That's my girl. "That was her home, and you torched it."

"That true, Hill?" I move in. "You add arson to your résumé?"

"It was just a house. And it wasn't like she needed that stuff. I did."

Deputy Douche sounds like he actually believes the crap he's spouting off. I can only imagine how Sarah Jo feels hearing this. That's her vindication, right here, but she cares for her client. You can't miss the concern and affection in her voice, and I know how my own elderly aunties and mother would feel about having a houseful of memories burned down around their ears. Violated, pissed off, and ready to rip the offender a new one before starting over, making new memories in a new place.

"You hear that?" Hunter makes a point of looking around. I spot a couple of phones up, out, and recording as Deputy Douche spills his secrets.

"Uh-huh. That's ten to twenty right there, for attempted kidnapping. And we've got ourselves an arson."

That's one problem sorted.

I turn to look for Sarah Jo. She's making a break for it.

Again.

PICK

I'M NOT the kind of person who sits around and waits. I don't need closure. I don't need to rehash what's happened or how I feel about it. Apparently, that's something Sarah Jo and I have in common because she starts moving away from our showdown with the good deputy. She's an amazing woman, and she's got grit. Brains. Beauty. The whole package, if I'm being honest. But I really don't want her to walk out on me now. I want her to talk to with me. To walk *into* my arms and let me wrap her up and love her. I hook a thumb in her zip-ties and gently swing her to a halt.

She stops since she has no choice and my heart falls. I've always thought that was some kind of expression, but I swear I feel the stupid, hopeful thing plummet from my ribs to my steel-toes. I have a moment of sheer panic as I consider the odds of her sticking out the summer.

She shifts her gaze from my face to the point where we're connected, the tied up, plastic, not-so-kinky point. The moment is far less romantic than I'd been hoping for. "What?"

"You don't think we should talk now? Or maybe you should offer up a thank-you?"

I have other suggestions, but I don't think she's in the mood to jump my bones right now.

"Okay." She looks cautious about the two of us having a conversation. I'll cut her some slack, seeing as how she's just had a really bad day. I'm no psychologist, but getting assaulted at work and then forcibly dragged away has to leave a mark. She seems okay, but Sarah Jo generally acts like showing any kind of vulnerability is a crime.

"Thank you," she continues in a prissy voice that makes me want to kiss her. Or paddle her butt. Choosing between the two right now is difficult. "Cut me loose."

She shoves her wrists at me, and I discover I have a mean side. I'm not in the mood for her orders. In fact, I think it's my turn to do some order-giving.

"Mmmm," I say. "I don't think so. Not yet."

"Pick—"

It's so cute the way she thinks she's in a position to demand things. The way I see it, her wrists may be tied up, but so is my heart. My head. Pick an organ and it's one hundred percent team Make This Woman Love Me.

"No." I repeat my refusal just so we're clear and run my hand down her arm. I might need to touch her for another century or six, just to make sure she's in one piece. She's not the only one who's had a bad day.

She frowns. "Is that the only word you know tonight?"

"Probably not." I can't hold back the smile tugging at my mouth. Her answering glare informs me in no uncertain terms that grinning is just fuel for the fire as far as she's concerned. "I'd like to hear that you're okay. Maybe you could tell me that."

She starts walking, and I fall into step beside her. The boys don't need my help babysitting Hill while they wait for a bona fide law enforcement official to show up.

She shakes her wrists at me. "I'd be better if you untied me."

She really doesn't like those ties. I'll bet she's running options in her head. In another two minutes, she'll have a Plan A, a Plan B, and possibly a Plan C for getting shed of them. I have to act fast.

"Maybe." I throw an arm around her, pulling her into my side. I think she fits perfectly.

She gives, just a little. "I'm okay."

"I'd like to see that for myself, honey."

When her feet slow down, because her stubborn side is clearly kicking in again, I swing her up into my arms. This feels right, having her cozied up against my chest. The way she wriggles, though, she doesn't share my opinion. I tighten my hold because I'll never drop her.

"Put me down," she snaps.

See? We're back to orders yet again. Sarah Jo loves orders—as long as she's the one giving them.

"You know how many years you took off my life tonight, Sarah Jo? When I heard you hollering, all I could think was that maybe I'd be too late. That maybe I wouldn't get there in time."

She shoots me a dirty look. "Believe me, I had the same concern."

"And that's another problem," I continue, my arms tightening briefly. "I'll always come when you need me, but you don't believe that. You want to handle everything on your own. What's wrong with letting someone else have your back?"

"I like standing on my own two feet," she shoots right back.

"You don't trust me," I counter.

She shakes her head. "That's not it."

"Really?" I look down at her and her pretty, stubborn face. "Because I practically had to pull the details about Hill from you."

She sucks in a breath. Exhales noisily. "I don't like not being in control."

"We could practice," I suggest. "Or take turns. Every other day could be Sarah Jo Day. You could think about staying."

Here. With me.

Does that sound stupid? God, she's everything I never knew I needed, and the way she stares up at me makes me want to beat my chest and swear I can be whoever and whatever she needs. As long as she takes a chance. On me.

On *us.*

She bites her lip, but she doesn't say anything. She doesn't deny that she's got every intention of leaving. Now that she's not starring front and center on Thad's most wanted list, she'll pack up and go.

And take my heart with her.

I do some fast thinking while I carry her to my RV. When we reach the trailer, I shift her in my arms and reach for the door. Hesitate.

"I need to tell you something." She rolls her eyes, but I keep talking. Sometimes, all you can do is dig a line in the ground and hope like hell the fire doesn't jump it. Sometimes, *all* you have is hope. "I love you, and I'd like to take you inside and show you. Or talk about it. Or just make plans for what we're going to do together for the next sixty years or so."

I'm holding my breath, waiting for her response. Just standing here on the steps to my RV, holding her tight in my arms, is about as close to heaven as I'm ever getting.

She chews on her lower lip. "You want to talk?"

"Sure." I drop a kiss on her forehead. Now I'm hoping that's a down payment on about a million more kisses. "If you're ready to listen to me. But I'd also like to show you that loaning someone else some of your self-control doesn't have to suck."

She looks at the closed door. "Take me inside," she says. That's not a yes—but it's not a no, either. I'll take what I can get.

I carry her inside the RV and kick the door shut behind us. It'll take a moment for my eyes to adjust, but I can find the bed with my eyes closed, even carrying precious cargo. I've walked this path hundreds of times, half-dead on my feet after days in the field. I set her down in the center of the mattress and flip on a light.

She promptly rolls over, shoving her wrists up at me. "Now untie me."

She's sprawled on my bed, on her knees, hands bound behind her. My head can't decide if I should try for a romantic heart-to-heart or just skip ahead to a very filthy happily-ever-after. I have such a dirty mind. Her mussed-up, trussed-up look is the most erotic thing I've ever seen. She's all long legs, her shorts riding up her ass and her hair tumbled around her face. She looks like she's just got out of bed, and it's a good look for her.

"Give me a minute." I sound hoarse. "You don't think you could enjoy this some? Because it's really, really working for me."

She wiggles her wrists at me. "You like having me tied up?"

"I like having you trust me," I say. "The tied-up thing is just an added bonus."

"Does this mean I get to tie you up tomorrow?"

I should have raided Deputy Douche's supply of zip-ties. How come I've never bought a silk necktie?

"If you promise to be very, very nice to me."

She giggles. She actually fucking giggles.

I think… she might like me. This. *Us.*

I gently press her down on her stomach. "You're making it damned hard to behave."

I press against her back, giving her a taste of my weight. The move traps her wrists between us, and her fingers brush first my stomach and then my dick as she wriggles. Not a *no* kind of wriggle, but *a yes let me get closer* move.

I don't have any fancy words. I haven't planned for this. I don't have roses, a Hallmark verse, or even a plan. "Stay with me? I'm a hotshot when you deserve a prince, but I'm good at my job. I'll always be able to take care of you."

"Idiot," she whispers. I believe that could be interpreted as *sexist, stupid guy who thinks I'll be his Suzy Homemaker.* She doesn't get it. I just want her to be Sarah Jo—but *with* me.

"You might want to be careful," I whisper, "passing out insults when you're the one with your hands tied behind your back."

I brush my mouth against her neck, giving her a series of little kisses. My dick is doing an excellent imitation of an iron bar, but he'll have to wait. I'm just hoping it's not forever.

"I don't need anyone to take care of me," she says slowly.

"True," I agree, and kiss her ear. She makes that husky, moaning gasp I love so much. "But will you let me?"

Sarah Jo being Sarah Jo, she promptly counters. She should have been a lawyer instead of a camp cook. "You going to let *me* take care of *you*?"

I think about that for a moment, while I kiss my way down her neck again.

"Sure," I say finally, nipping lightly at her shoulder. "Why wouldn't I want that? That's what partners do, Sarah Jo. They look out for each other. It's not a question of *you can't*. It's about *I want to*."

Convince her.

"You know what a hot zone is?" I trace my fingers along her neck and do a little more kissing while I wait for her answer. When she shakes her head, I explain. "When a fire really gets going, you can only get so close before someone gets burned. We keep the firefighters out of that zone so they all stay safe."

"Are you saying you want to cool things down?"

"No, honey. I'm saying I want to stand between you and the flames. Let go of your control, just for me. Let me do this for you."

"Let go," she repeats cautiously. Her fingers flex between us, and it's my turn to bite back a groan as her fingertips swipe over my dick. She could be clueless about what she's touching. Knowing my Sarah Jo, however, it's probably part of a devious master plan. That teasing brush of her, just a light caress against my jeans, makes me hard. Hungry. I want this woman something fierce, but I also want more than one more night of hot sex. I want all of Sarah Jo.

"Let me show you," I suggest. "Let me take charge tonight."

SARAH JO

Pick is a big, sexy, *stubborn* bastard. I flex my wrists, but the plastic ties have even less give than the man wrapped around me. He wants something from me. He wants love. He wants to love me and be loved in return. It's a sweet, sweet idea, this possibility of Pick caring for me like that. He'd make one hell of a partner.

If I'm honest, it would be easy to love him back.

It would also be scary as hell. I don't like being tied up or tied down. I definitely don't like not being in control. Loving this man would be like putting zip-ties on my heart, and it would be so easy for him to hurt me.

"Let's try this, honey." I don't miss the rough need in his voice. *This* apparently being sex while I'm tied up. I've never done kink before because it's never been my thing. I wriggle, trying to find some room to think that's not full of sexy hotshot, but he's not letting me put any space between us. Evidently, he's serious about this whole opening up and trusting thing.

One quick, hard tug of his hands, and my shorts and panties fly down my legs. He steps away from the bed for a moment, and then the rustle of clothing hitting the floor is followed by the dip of the mattress as he climbs right back beside me. That handful of seconds is enough for me to decide that *I* don't like waiting for *him* to decide what comes next; this is definitely not my kind of game.

When I try to roll over, however, a firm hand at the small of my back holds me in place.

"Stay put," he growls. "Right where you are."

Should I? *Can* I? I haven't been given the rulebook for this game, but it doesn't seem to matter. His hands arrange me gently, on my knees, facedown. Kinky sex it is.

Kinky sex with Pick, I remind myself.

"Yes," I say out loud. Yes to everything, yes to Pick.

He groans. "You know how pretty you look?"

I *look* exposed. I'm pretty darn sure of that. It's not enough for him, though. He parts my thighs, one big hand on each, gently pressing me further open. All the way, no holding back. Just me, him, the bed, and way too many emotions.

He touches me. No warning, just one thick finger sliding through my folds from bottom to top. All the way up my soaked slit until he finds my clit and pinches lightly.

I moan. *Oh, God.*

"You got something you want to say to me?"

"More?"

He repeats the caress, drawing his fingers through

my slickness again. "That, too."

"Untie me? I want to get my arms around you," I admit. "Maybe we can take turns having kinky sex tomorrow and just go for the vanilla, face-to-face stuff tonight?"

He swipes his pants from the floor, fishing for his utility knife. "Don't move."

I lie there, blinking a little because I'm finally right where I want to be. I don't want to leave. A quick slice of the blade, and my wrists pop apart. I roll, taking in the intent look on his face. His big hands rub at the red marks from the ties.

"Shit." He frowns. "I should have cut you free sooner."

"It's all right." And it is. I sort of want to cry and to yell and to climb all over that big body of his and make him feel the pleasure, too. Pick is my hot zone and my safety zone, and I'm more than ready to spend fire season—and forever—in his arms. We'll take turns being in control—or letting go. It's going to be okay, even if I don't get it right the first time. All I have to is practice—and trust Pick.

And I do. I trust him with every tied up, too scared, not quite sure enough inch of me, starting with me head and ending with my heart. I love him, and he loves me.

"I'm okay," I repeat.

He frames my face with his hands and kisses me, a hot, sweet kiss that makes me heat up. "In that case—"

"Yeah," I say, laughing. "You've got something to finish."

"One thing first." His face, watching mine, is suddenly serious. "I don't want to be finished here. I just want you to know that. Stay or go, that's your call, but you should know that I'll be here waiting for you. You don't need to say anything, but I needed you to hear that."

"You don't mind? If I'm not in the mood for talking?"

"Honey"—he eases his hand along my shoulder—"this isn't about what I want. You say what you need to say. Whatever you've got, you give it to me."

"That's it?"

He slides his fingers into the tangled hair at the back of my neck, urging me forward for another kiss. It's a fabulous idea—one of the best he's had all night.

"Probably not," he admits. "We're going to fight. Kiss and make up."

I walk my fingers up his chest. "Maybe it's time for

that kissing part."

"Uh-huh." I can feel the low rumble of his laughter beneath my cheek. "I could do that."

"I love you." I say the words quietly, but I know he hears me.

"Say you'll stay the summer. The fall. I've got four seasons, and every one of them is for you."

"I could do that." I pull his head toward mine, wanting his kiss. "You still looking for that hot zone, hotshot?"

He smiles slowly. "Could be."

"Then sign me up. I'm all yours."

ABOUT THE AUTHOR

After ten years of graduate school and too many degrees, Anne Marsh escaped to become a technical writer. When not planted firmly in front of the laptop translating Engineer into English, Anne enjoys gardening, running (even if it's just to the 7-11 for slurpees), and reading books curled up with her kids. The best part of writing romance, however, is finally being able to answer the question: "So… what do you do with a PhD in Slavic Languages and Literatures?" She lives in Northern California with her husband, two kids and four cats.

Printed in Great Britain
by Amazon